On his lips her name was an erotic whisper

He lifted up his right hand, perhaps to touch her out-stretched arm. She would never know, for J.D.'s fingers brushed her breast and she forgot to breathe. The pain eased from his brow and his lips fell open. She had only to stop stroking his brow to end this accidental touch, but the want of it rose up like a craziness in her blood.

She couldn't seem to help herself. Memories of his kiss those long months ago made her weak with longing. She'd been able to shut out those memories back in Seattle, but not here, not living with him as she was, as if he were her husband and she his bride, twenty-four hours a day.

Even hiding as they were, him wounded and her dogged by her past, even with a maniac on their trail, *this* was what she wanted…J.D.'s hand on her breast, stroking her, cupping her, all so slowly with such care and erotic sensibility that she could have died.

"Look at me, Annie," he whispered.

As she dragged her gaze to him, he took her hand and put it low on on his body, to the one sweet liberty she hadn't already stolen. "Give us a chance, Ann," he groaned. "Won't you give us a chance?"

Dear Harlequin Intrigue Reader,

You wanted MORE MEN OF MYSTERY by Gayle Wilson—now you've got 'em! Gayle's stories about these sexy undercover agents have become one of Harlequin Intrigue's most popular ongoing series. We are as impressed by her outstanding talent as you, her readers, and are thrilled to feature her special brand of drama again in *Her Private Bodyguard* (#561). Look for two MORE titles in August and November 2000.

Also available this month, *Protecting His Own* (#562) by Molly Rice, an emotional story about the sanctity of family and a man's basic need to claim what's his.

There's no more stronger bond than that of blood. And Chance Quarrels is determined to see no harm come to the little daughter he never knew he had as Patricia Rosemoor continues her SONS OF SILVER SPRINGS miniseries with *The Lone Wolf's Child* (#563).

Finally, veteran Harlequin Intrigue author Carly Bishop takes you to a cloistered Montana community with a woman and an undercover cop posing as husband and wife. The threat from a killer is real, but so is their simmering passion. Which one is more dangerous...? Find out in *No Bride But His* (#564), a LOVERS UNDER COVER story.

Pick up all four for variety, for excitement—because you're ready for a thrill!

Sincerely,

Denise O'Sullivan
Associate Senior Editor
Harlequin Intrigue

No Bride But His
Carly Bishop

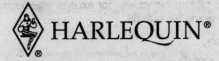

HARLEQUIN®

TORONTO • NEW YORK • LONDON
AMSTERDAM • PARIS • SYDNEY • HAMBURG
STOCKHOLM • ATHENS • TOKYO • MILAN • MADRID
PRAGUE • WARSAW • BUDAPEST • AUCKLAND

ISBN 0-373-22564-4

NO BRIDE BUT HIS

Copyright © 2000 by Cheryl McGonigle

This edition published by arrangement with Harlequin Books S.A.

® and TM are trademarks of the publisher. Trademarks indicated with
® are registered in the United States Patent and Trademark Office, the
Canadian Trade Marks Office and in other countries.

Visit us at www.eHarlequin.com

Printed in U.S.A.

ABOUT THE AUTHOR

Carly Bishop's novels are praised for their "sensuality, riveting emotional appeal and first-class suspense." She was a RITA Award finalist in 1996 for her Harlequin Intrigue novel *Reckless Lover*, and she's won numerous awards and critical acclaim throughout her ten-year writing career. Carly lives in Colorado and regularly uses the great Rocky Mountains as the backdrop in her stories.

Books by Carly Bishop

HARLEQUIN INTRIGUE
170—FUGITIVE HEART
232—FALLING STARS
314—HOT BLOODED
319—BREATHLESS
323—HEART THROB
357—RECKLESS LOVER
370—THE SOULMATE
394—SHADOW LOVER
440—ANGEL WITH AN ATTITUDE
454—WATCH OVER ME
497—McQUAID'S JUSTICE
538—NO BABY BUT MINE
564—NO BRIDE BUT HIS

Don't miss any of our special offers. Write to us at the following address for information on our newest releases.

Harlequin Reader Service
U.S.: 3010 Walden Ave., P.O. Box 1325, Buffalo, NY 14269
Canadian: P.O. Box 609, Fort Erie, Ont. L2A 5X3

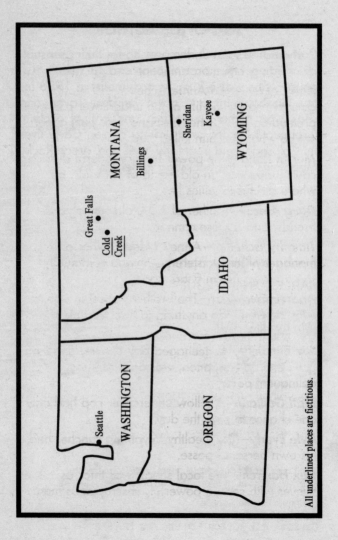

All underlined places are fictitious.

CAST OF CHARACTERS

J. D. Thorne—An undercover cop working to dismantle a lethal organization of vigilantes.

Ann Calder—Aka Annie Tschetter, the Seattle detective saved the life of the undercover cop by pretending he was her husband. Her past might yet be what gets him killed....

Martin Rand—The power-hungry federal district court judge was an old friend of Thorne's, but where did his loyalties lie?

Doug Ames—Another of J.D.'s old schoolyard friends, and a loose cannon.

Timothy Tschetter—Anne's oldest brother and manager of the cloistered Montana community she ran away from years ago.

Andreas Tschetter—The brother closest in age to Ann, he would do anything to help his little sister and her husband....

Jaz Zimmer—The teenaged boy, the tiny son Ann gave over for adoption, was on a reckless, delinquent path.

Matt Guiliani—A fellow undercover cop had only one chance to save the day.

Kyle Everly—The wealthy Wyoming rancher had his own personal posse.

Dex Hanifen—The local sheriff was thick as thieves with certain powerful, unscrupulous men.

Chapter One

CNBC Special Report, correspondent from the scene, Superior Court of King County:

"As Detective Ann Calder takes the stand today in the trial of former Seattle detective Ross Vorees, we are only beginning to appreciate the penetration of vigilante justice into our legitimate law enforcement agencies by members of the so-called 'TruthSayers.' Here is what we now know.

"Assistant U.S. attorney John Grenallo had long been sabotaging the efforts of his own undercover team, dedicated to dismantling the TruthSayers threat.

"It started five years ago when Justice Department photographer Kirsten McCourt caught on video the execution-style murder by Chet Loehman, head of the vigilante organization, of a young rancher. That evidence was destroyed. Before his suicide some weeks back, John Grenallo was charged with this conspiracy to thwart justice.

"This trial follows on the indictment of former Seattle detective Ross Vorees with the murder of one Burton Rawlings, who had come into possession of *copies on computer diskettes of the photographic evidence believed destroyed five years ago.*

"Rawlings unwittingly alerted the TruthSayers to his find, and they, in turn, kidnapped Ms. McCourt's four-year-old son, demanding the evidence in exchange for little Christo McCourt's life.

"Rawlings revealed the whereabouts of the evidence and, according to the prosecution, was then fatally shot by Detective Vorees.

"We now surmise Ross Vorees intended to assume control of the TruthSayers vigilante organization himself.

"Whatever control Vorees exercises will be from a prison cell. His conviction in Wyoming for the murder of his rival, Chet Loehman, came swiftly. Meanwhile, his trial for the murder of Burton Rawlings has entered the last hours for the prosecution with the testimony of the petite, steely-eyed redhead, Detective Ann Calder...

"SO, MS. CALDER. Let us clarify, shall we, what it is your testimony this morning was about."

Seated in the witness stand of the King County Superior Court, facing one of the premier defense attorneys in the nation, Ann knew Morton Downey's intent was a far cry from clarifying anything.

Burton Rawlings was dead and Ross Vorees had murdered him, but the evidence in this case was hopelessly circumstantial. The fact that she had seen Vorees on the police practice range with an unusual handgun identical in model and appearance to the murder weapon wasn't going to make the prosecutor's shoddy case.

She matched the defense attorney's polite tone.

"How may I assist you, Mr. Downey?" She would assist to the extent that he clarified.

He shot her a look. "When Kirsten McCourt came to report hearing a murder threat over her son Christo's child monitor, you were the one taking the complaint?"

"Yes. I was the detective who took Kirsten McCourt's statement."

"And you've testified that you soon realized, Ms. Calder, that this murder threat might well have something to do with the TruthSayers and Chet Loehman, head honcho of the so-called vigilante organization. Leaving aside, for the moment, the leap in logic—"

"There was no leap, Mr. Downey. I knew—"

"You knew, didn't you, Ms. Calder, that you would have to turn the case over to Detective Vorees, isn't that—"

"I prefer to be addressed as *Detective,* as well, Mr. Downey."

"And I prefer an answer to my question."

Ann squared her slight shoulders. She stood only five-four and weighed a hundred and fifteen pounds, but though she had taken down men three times her size, perps and their attorneys routinely underestimated her.

If Ross Vorees's high-powered mouthpiece intended to intimidate her, he would be disappointed.

She held Downey's fiery, accusing gaze and let the silence stretch out for no other reason than to show the menacing attorney what she was made of. The judge himself intervened, directing her to answer the question before she spoke again.

"I referred the case to the defendant. Yes." She would not refer to a convicted murderer as "detective.'' In the wake of his conviction in Wyoming, Vorees had been relieved of duty. ''I knew the defendant would in turn have to hand Ms. McCourt over to the U.S. Attorney's TruthSayers undercover operations.''

''Consisting of?''

''Garrett Weisz, Matt Guiliani and—'' Her throat felt suddenly tight, her composure tilted, vulnerable at the mere thought of J.D. Thorne. He had laid his own life on the line for his friend, Garrett, and lightened Kirsten's unbearable load with his kindness.

Ann had never seen the kind of loyalty she thought defined him best, exemplified his actions. Such a rare and old-fashioned thing nowadays, that kind of fealty. A thing sensed, understood, hardly mentioned, priceless and unlike her history, littered with broken ties.

J.D. had kissed her and she had kissed him back, only once, the night Christo McCourt was recovered from the TruthSayer kidnappers, but she was ever after altered. Not herself.

Never herself again.

He'd gazed at her from the start with breathtaking admiration, as if he could tell from looking at her exactly what fires of hell she had been through in her life.

''*And?*'' Downey hounded her.

She finished her sentence. ''And J.D. Thorne.''

''And you resented the very devil out of that, all those men?''

''Excuse me?'' In her lapse, against the tide of emotion, of heat flaring inside her, she hadn't heard Downey's question.

''Spare me the attitude, Ms. Calder,'' Downey

snapped, somehow having missed a beat himself, somehow mistaking her confusion for disdain. "You resented having to turn the case over to Detective Vorees. You resented it bitterly, in fact. You were the detective who caught the case, after all."

She wouldn't fall into his verbal trap. "Yes, I was the detective, but no, I don't resent having—"

"The truth is, you harbor a powerful resentment toward Detective Vorees in particular—"

"No."

"—and toward men in general. Isn't that so, Ms. Calder?"

"No, Mr. Downey, it is not."

"No?" he mocked. "You're what…thirty-two? Are you married, Ms. Calder? Have you ever been?"

"No."

"In a relationship?"

"Not recently."

"Are you even dating, Ms. Calder?"

"Badgering and pointless, Your Honor!" the prosecutor, Warren Remster, intervened, mechanically tossing a pencil onto his stack of notes, as if reluctant to create the appearance of having to defend her. "Detective Calder's personal life isn't—"

"Withdrawn," Downey interrupted. "We'll come back to that soon enough. Now, Ms. Calder, what was your first opportunity to examine the murder weapon?"

"I saw the weapon in the ballistics lab."

Downey raised his eyebrows and puffed out his chest in surprise. "You went looking?"

"Yes."

"Were you assigned to this case? Have any official reason whatsoever to go looking?"

"No."

"No. In fact, you heard through the grapevine that the weapon was a Colt .357 magnum, isn't that so?"

Ann nodded, agreeing.

"I'm sorry, Ms. Calder. I didn't hear your answer."

"My answer is yes." She went through the specifications she had noted, the length of barrel, type of bluing, uniqueness of the custom ivory-inlaid grip. "This was a singular weapon, Mr. Downey. Definitely high-end, not standard-issue."

"But again those are all details you might have heard on the grapevine, which makes your timing in coming forward with what you knew just a little suspect, wouldn't you agree?"

She had argued this weakness in the case herself with the prosecution team. If the investigating detectives had come to her and asked if she knew anyone who owned a custom .357 magnum *before* it was revealed to be the murder weapon, the result would have been the same, but the defense spin would have been impossible. She *had* seen Ross Vorees using that weapon, or its exact match, on the practice range, but she had come forward with that information on her own—which in Morton Downey's universe made her suspect.

"Were you looking for a way to frame my client, Detective Calder, or did you just take advantage—"

"Objection!" Remster bellowed. "Your Honor—"

"Overruled." Scowling, the judge shut down the protest. "You cannot have been unaware of what your witness knew and when she knew it, Counsel, and yet you put her on the stand. I'm going to grant the defense every latitude here.''

"Your Honor,'' the prosecutor protested, "the integrity of the witness is unimpeachable.''

"Because she's a cop?'' The judge shook his head. "Maybe in some alternate reality, sir, but not in my courtroom.''

The judge looked away as if to indicate Downey should continue, instead launching himself into a tirade that made Ann's heart sink a little lower. The city had been rocked with police-corruption issues for a couple of years. The prosecutors had believed that because Ann had helped expose John Grenallo's role in the kidnapping of Christo McCourt, her credibility was rock-solid.

The judge wasn't buying. "Cut to the chase, Mr. Downey.''

Pleased with himself, the defense attorney started in again. "Ms. Calder. You live in a three-story building you own and operate as a halfway house for battered women and—''

"—runaway children, yes.''

"Almost…communally. Could we agree on that?''

She doubted very much that Downey had any conception of the way she lived or what he was saying. "Yes, Mr. Downey, we could agree upon that.''

"With a shared kitchen and living area?''

"Yes. But I have my own quarters—''

"What?'' Downey interrupted. "Seven—''

"—seven hundred square feet to call my own?'' Ann snapped, knowing exactly where the defendant's counsel was headed. "Yes, Mr. Downey, that is how

I live." Even after all these years, seven hundred square feet to herself still felt palatial.

She watched Downey close in on the witness stand. On her. "So, Ms....excuse me, *Detective* Calder, tell me. Please. You take these poor, battered souls into your own home, not occasionally, but as a matter of course." Ann supposed if Downey wanted to, he could make Mother Teresa look foolish. "You *live* with the effects of violence perpetrated by men against women and children. I can't imagine how you do that. How do you manage it? How do you keep so pure a heart that you harbor virtually no resentment toward men?"

Ann's chin went up. He could mock her until the saints came marching home. She would not be shamed. She would not wither or come undone under anyone else's opinions of her. She'd made that decision before she knew how to put it into words. "Unlike you, Mr. Downey, I am able to separate—"

"Move to strike as nonresponsive," Downey interrupted, spitting the words.

"Move to strike this entire cross-examination," the prosecutor protested, rising wearily from his chair. "Is counsel seriously suggesting Detective Calder's living arrangements have anything to do with her observation of the murder weapon in the defendant's possession?"

"Mr. Prosecutor," the judge said in a lethally soft tone, "we are talking a weapon *like* the murder weapon. And I believe I've made myself clear. The defense is entitled to an examination of your witness's motives in coming forward with what she knew. On the other hand, Mr. Downey—" he turned to the defense attorney "—my patience is wearing exceedingly thin. That Detective Calder is a detective does not make her honest. That she serves the community by offering her home up as a halfway house does not make her a manhater, nor does it remotely imply a vendetta against your client.''

Downey bowed his neck. ''Your Honor, Ms. Calder's motives—''

''*Detective* Calder's motives, Counsel,'' the judge interrupted, ''can now be judged by the jury. You have only one question left of this witness. I'll ask it.'' He turned in his chair to look down at Ann. ''Detective, I remind you that you are under oath. Were you aware before you knew the make of the gun used to kill Burton Rawlings that your fellow detective, Ross Vorees, owned such a weapon?''

Ann straightened. ''Yes.''

The judge nodded. ''Anything more, Mr. Downey?'' he asked, his tone implying there had better be very little else.

For a long moment Downey stood glaring at her. ''That's your story?''

''Yes.'' She saw for a split second regret in the shape of his lips. He would have been far better off dismissing her without any cross-examination at all.

''And you're sticking with it?'' he mocked.

She almost felt sorry for him. How could he know? By the age of four, she had confronted in the assembly of her elders far sterner stuff than Morton Downey could even begin to fathom.

Her ''story'' wasn't, but it could have been a bold-faced lie, and still he would not have rattled her. ''Yes, Mr. Downey. That's my story and I am sticking with it.''

WATCHING MORTON DOWNEY'S cross-examination of Ann Calder on the closed-circuit monitor in his office, despite the smattering of laughter in the courtroom, J. D. Thorne wasn't amused.

He'd tried to keep his sense of humor.

He'd really tried very hard. He meant to keep his cool. He had to remind himself twenty times a day, once per hour every waking hour, that there had been a time, butting heads with Garrett Weisz, that he had wanted to be in charge of the TruthSayers undercover ops.

He was in charge now, though "undercover" no longer applied, and God was almost certainly laughing. His prayers had been answered, and now J.D. was more feared and avoided than all the cops in the Internal Investigations Section rolled together.

The IIS hatchetmen pitied *him*.

Still he had kept his sense of humor. He believed in what he was doing. Secret vigilantes operating behind the scenes at virtually every level of law enforcement had to be identified, investigated, relieved of duty and criminally charged.

They had to be stopped.

The deeper he got into his investigations, the thicker the thieves, so to speak. John Grenallo had hanged himself rather than stand before his wife and kids and God and the community he'd served for nine years and admit that he had given away the place where his undercover agents had stashed Christo McCourt for safekeeping. Except, J.D. wasn't buying. The theory imparted a greater decency to John Grenallo than J.D. was willing to allow.

He couldn't even imagine what story Grenallo

must have had to tell himself to justify the act of aiding and abetting the kidnap of a four-year-old boy.

Then there were the vigilante beat cops, meting out their own brand of justice, chalking up the murders of perps who'd beaten the system to drive-by shootings.

The presumption of innocence turned on its head. If his uncle, the only father figure J.D. had ever known, hadn't been court-martialed in a painstaking frame-up, only to be exonerated fifteen excruciating years later, maybe J.D. wouldn't feel so personally offended.

Or maybe he would. His uncle Jess had been a marine, and J.D. was raised hard-core. *Semper fi.*

In the wake of his investigations, the question had come up like so much dirty laundry: When Thorne was done, would there be one cop left standing?

Even when he had been lampooned in the *Sun-Times* for a lantern-jawed zealot tossing the baby out with the bathwater—the least offensive of half a dozen such political cartoons—J.D. had kept his sense of humor.

But his heart grew heavier by the day. If someone had told him there would come a time when he wouldn't have the stomach to do his job, he'd have laughed.

He wasn't laughing now, watching the trial on the closed-circuit monitor. Watching Ann, his guts closed up tight as could be.

After she finished, having testified as well as it was possible to do given what she had to say, J.D. snatched the insulated sheepskin vest off the back of his ladderback chair and shrugged into it on his way out of the building. Passing the security checkpoints, he pushed through the door, maneuvered around a gaggle of press members, reaching the parking lot and his beloved, refurbished lime-green Camaro in time to escape even the most dogged reporters.

He zipped off the lot and into the midafternoon snarl of traffic, but he had no hope of dodging his own thoughts.

He hadn't seen Ann Calder in months. He knew she sometimes went to dinner with Garrett and Kirsten. He knew she often took Christo to the movies. The little kid was so enamored of her wide gray eyes and the halo of red hair—far too unruly, in J.D.'s opinion, for the forties-era roll she wore at her nape—that Christo intended to marry her when he grew up.

And he knew that Matt Guiliani, the third member of the crack undercover team to have rescued Christo, dropped by her place with Wag the Dog in tow a couple of times a week. He knew because Guiliani, who had been removed from the TruthSayers investigations to keep some semblance of low profile, made a point of calling J.D. for no other discernible purpose than to toss into the conversation that he'd spent some hours with Ann.

Guiliani, of course, thought J.D. was all kinds of a fool for staying away, and he didn't keep that opinion to himself either.

J.D. knew about the halfway house too. He didn't pretend to understand Ann's motives for sinking everything she owned and earned into supporting the place—or why she'd chosen to live like that. Not even Guiliani had a theory to spout on the subject, but Ann Calder had earned the bedrock loyalty of every woman and child she had ever sheltered in her home. Some of those kids were adults now, and helped her out all the time. All J.D. knew was that Ann Calder made forever-kind of friends out of everyone she met.

Everyone but him.

They couldn't very well *be* friends, or only just friends. Not the way the very air between them pulsed. Not in an aeon would the kiss they shared after Christo's rescue be half-forgotten.

They hadn't really fit. It hadn't really mattered.

He was six-two to her five-four, but he'd lifted her right off her feet, and the deep coursing thrill of her full rounded breasts flattened against his chest, the touch of her small, sweet hands to his face, was only preamble to the kiss.

He lurched through traffic, cutting in and out of lanes just to give some vent to his frustration. What ought to be a hazy, fading pleasant memory was instead a vivid, glowing ember too hot to touch, too incendiary to contain in a cozy, festive package called friendship, and before their lips had parted, they'd both known it.

Before Christo fell asleep that night, Ann had backed off, bailed out, begged J.D. not to come around her when they returned to Seattle. She believed he would sooner or later find himself disappointed in her, and she was unwilling to arrive at that moment.

But unlike Morton Downey with his eagle eye and killer instinct, J.D. with his heart on his sleeve didn't miss her hesitation when she named him as one of the undercover team.

Not in an aeon, Ann.

The thought gave him an undeniably perverse

pleasure. It tore him up to be so many weeks out from one lone, heated kiss, still pining, still wanting, still seeing himself and his fears redeemed in her eyes, still coveting an unwilling woman with a will of iron.

She hadn't forgotten it either. Through the closed-circuit feed from the courtroom to his office, seeing her stumble so subtly even the predatory Morton Downey missed it, J.D. knew she wasn't as forgetful as she would like to be.

He had a will as well. Still, he didn't know what it would take for him to break the lamebrained promise he'd made to her that night not to seek her out. A man honored his promises.

All but the lamebrained ones. Ask Guiliani.

If it was only the kiss, he'd have had a chance of forgetting, but it wasn't. There was a gentleness about Ann, an integrity, a well of strength and compassion that invited all sorts of confession that he knew must draw as many men to her as the women she sheltered.

Something else drew him. Something hard and unforgiving in her nature, something that reminded him what an unforgiving bastard he was himself. Something that suggested she knew what he was about. Knew and understood and *believed* some things were unforgivable. The kiss was about more than an instant, overwhelming attraction.

That kiss was about two souls forged in fires hotter than hell, rising out of the ashes together.

Chapter Two

It took him nearly an hour through the afternoon traffic to get onto Mercer Island where his oldest friend Martin Rand lived on a multimillion-dollar waterfront property. Then he saw a black urban assault vehicle, otherwise known as an SUV, parked at the far end of Rand's circular driveway, nearly hidden by thick, lush ferns and evergreen bushes.

Feeling peevish, bent-out, J.D. turned off the ignition of his Camaro, plugged the license-plate numbers into the handheld unit connected to a statewide computer network and sat there waiting for a response.

A few seconds later a name came up.

The Honorable Federal District Court Judge Martin Rand, on a three-month sabbatical, was entertaining Douglas Andrew Ames. An uneasiness set J.D.'s teeth on edge. He and Rand had grown up with Doug Ames and Kyle Everly.

Everly was the quiet one, somehow accumulating the money for their sorties into trouble. Rand conned the adults and collected favors like some Mafia don, J.D. worked out all the angles should they be caught, and Ames…

Ames had been the token nutcase juvenile delinquent, especially after his mother had asphyxiated in a fire at the diner she owned. As far as J.D. was concerned, Ames would always be a loose cannon, even if he'd reinvented himself as a real-estate tycoon after years working for the gun lobby in Washington, D.C.

He didn't like Ames. Maybe he never had. He'd come here because Rand always made a good sounding board and had a talent for raising another perspective. That kind of conversation wouldn't happen in front of Ames. J.D. was about to start up the Camaro and drive off when Rand opened the intricately carved front door of the ranch-style house and walked out with Ames.

J.D. got out of the Camaro as if he'd only just arrived and started up the walk. Ames's boyishly handsome face, his teeth clinched around an unlit cigar, lit up. "J.D.! This is a surprise. Didn't know you showed your face in public at all these days." He jabbed J.D. in a sidearmed punch to the shoulder. "How the hell are you?"

Instantly put off, J.D. returned the phony gesture, then cut a look to Rand. "Got no complaints."

"Really? Keeping the streets safe for decent folk hasn't ever looked less appealing, frankly," Ames cracked. "If I were you—" he winked "—I'd crawl in a hole and pull it in over me, if you know what I mean."

"Not exactly." For so little provocation, a joke really, J.D. felt his neck hairs going on end. "Why don't you spell it out for me, Dougie?"

Ames flushed. "When you're out there poking

sticks at wild animals, you better know sooner or later one of them is going to—"

"Back off, Ames." Rand cut him off and stuck himself physically between J.D. and a sore fist. "You too, J.D. Everyone's concerned about your safety. It isn't exactly a secret that there are cops out there willing to stick a shiv in your heart just for bragging rights."

"Look," Ames placated too easily, spreading his hands wide. "No harm, no foul, huh, buddy? Come on, J.D. We go back a long ways. I was just telling Rand I'm having a poker party on my houseboat next week. Why don't you come? Do you good to get away for a few hours."

A cold rain began to fall, a nasty drizzle. J.D. felt the fight drain out of him. He had no real beef with Ames. Nothing current, only history. "I don't think so, Doug."

Ames bit too hard into the cigar and snatched it out of his mouth, spitting little bits of tobacco. "You've changed, J.D."

"Have I?"

"Yeah." Ames plucked a stubborn piece off his lip. "There was a time when you knew who your friends were. Now—" He broke off. "I'm out of here." He strode off to the far end of the circular driveway, then called out as he opened the car door. "You take care, J.D. You've lost your way." J.D. had nothing to say. He wondered if the reason was that Doug Ames was not far off the mark.

They turned toward the house. Rand cocked an eyebrow as Ames's SUV roared off down the street. Still wordless, he opened the carved door and headed across the foyer into the living room to a wet bar fashioned of teak. The room was filled with treasures from the Orient.

The silk Turkish carpet alone, alive with different colors at every angle over a dark varnished hardwood floor, had to have cost a small fortune. Rand played violin with an elite chamber-music group, and on an antique music stand sat a bow to match the quality of his own personal Stradivarius.

"Tilting at windmills again, J.D.?" Rand used an ivory-handled church key to crack open a couple of long-necked bottles of beer. "What's wrong with you?"

J.D. took the proffered bottle, scowling. Not for the first time he wondered if it was Ames in the thrall of Rand's power, or Rand's fascination with Ames's staggering amorality that kept them in the same orbit.

"Other than this bogus trial, you mean?"

"Windmills it is." Rand lifted his bottle. "To Don Quixote. May his spirit live forever."

"Forevermore," J.D. intoned darkly. He guzzled down half his own bottle, watching Rand, still a ringer for a younger Sean Connery, his black hair just beginning to acquire a few silver streaks.

Rand kicked off a pair of wildly expensive sandals, sank deep into a club chair and put his bare feet up on a cut-glass coffee table. "Don't you think Burton Rawlings is entitled to some justice?"

"Does a dead man get justice?" He shook his head. "Ann's testimony—"

"Ann, is it?"

J.D. glowered. He and Rand had known each other when they were both horny adolescents trading in baseball cards for girlie pinups. They were close, had always been close, but J.D. had not said one word about Ann Calder. What was there to say?

But Rand saw too much too well and put together the rest with an annoying accuracy. "Calder's testimony," J.D. intoned, "must be some kind of last-ditch effort—"

"To lose the case?"

J.D. felt himself doing a double take. He'd either not heard Rand right, or he wasn't in Kansas anymore. "What is that supposed to mean?"

"Come on, J.D. " Rand focused on his buffed and polished thumbnail scraping at the label on the bottle of beer before he finally met J.D.'s eyes. "Tell me you know it's only going to go downhill from here."

"Meaning what?" J.D. demanded. "The prosecutors are running scared?"

"Could be."

"Or not. Warren Remster's ego is—"

"The district attorney's ego" Rand interrupted, "isn't at stake, my friend. With this trial, the D.A. will have covered his backside from every direction. You, meanwhile, are butting your head against a brick wall that's being reinforced every minute Vorees's trial drags on."

"I am not backing off this investigation, Marty. I won't do it."

"For what," Rand snapped, leaning forward from the deep cushions of the club chair. "A handful of penny-ante obstruction charges?"

"Obstruction is the tip of the iceberg. We're talking kidnapping, murder, extortion. If Remster won't prosecute them, the feds will."

"You may know Vorees masterminded the kidnap of Christo McCourt, but you can't prove it, and that's the only case the feds have the jurisdiction to enter. Listen to me now, J.D., because you need to hear this. Warren Remster is prosecuting this case *because* it's a loser. For no other reason. If you're smart you'll get out while the getting is…possible.''

J.D. stiffened. The disparity between their respective positions had never troubled him. J.D. was in a place he'd always wanted to be, doing the work he'd been cut out to do. Rand wasn't more ambitious, only vastly more political. But for the first time, J.D. felt the power differential oozing from Rand like cold sweat out his pampered pores.

''You can't be serious.''

''I am not kidding you. Not for a second.'' Rand brought the long-necked bottle of beer to his lips and polished it off, never breaking eye contact. ''Mark my words.''

''There's always racketeering,'' J.D. said. ''Come to think of it, that's a fairly accurate description of the TruthSayers, and—''

''That won't happen. The feds will not intervene. It's over, J.D. *It's over.* Remster is only prosecuting Vorees so that when the case tanks, his decision not to prosecute the remainder of the TruthSayer cases will seem like a reasoned, thoughtful decision for the greater good of the community.''

J.D. knew, chapter and verse, the relevant section of the criminal code. A prosecuting attorney was entitled under the law to decline to prosecute, even when there existed technically sufficient evidence to proceed. The only reason necessary was the prosecutor's belief that to prosecute would serve no public purpose, or that it would defeat the intention of the laws in question.

Or, and this one was the ringer, if the result of prosecuting would decrease respect for the law.

So the TruthSayers had only to wrap themselves in their typical banner. They existed to *restore* respect for the law, to restore justice to a system gone soft on predators and criminals.

J.D. had never seen the statute invoked, or imagined, before now, how it might be exploited. He could almost have sympathized if the prosecutors were afraid for their own lives to proceed, but this…this took hubris to another level altogether.

And with a sudden, sick certainty, J.D. was terribly afraid that the strategy had trickled down to Warren Remster from the lips of the Honorable Martin Rand.

He sat forward on the oxblood leather sofa, his feet on the exquisite Turkish carpet expensive enough to feed the women and children in Ann Calder's halfway house for a year or more. With infinite care, to counter the urge to smash something, J.D. set his empty beer bottle on a coaster made of brass.

"Remember when you learned in advance the Senate vote confirming your appointment to the federal district court? You had this cat-ate-the-canary grin on your face and I said, 'The bench is yours, isn't it?' Remember what you said to me?"

"Yeah." Rand put on a nostalgic grin. "I said I could tell you the results of the vote, but then I'd have to kill you."

J.D. didn't so much as blink. "Maybe you will after all."

Rand paled. "Don't be a jackass."

But now, his suspicions began to take on a life all their own. "Tell me about John Grenallo's suicide."

Rand's wide, handsome forehead creased in con-

tempt. "Tell you what, J.D.? The man was a mega-
lomaniac caught with his pants down—and worse, a
coward. He hung himself because he couldn't face
the shame of his wife and kids knowing he'd personally thrown Christo McCourt to the wolves."

"Nah." J.D. shook his head. His heart felt thick
and plodding, numb to have stumbled over the suspicion that his oldest friend could be the deepest
mole, the maestro behind the scenes of the Truth-
Sayers conspiracy. "I'm thinking Grenallo was too
smart to take that fall. He could easily have laid the
blame for leaking Christo's location at Ross Vorees's
feet."

"That's ridiculous." But the Honorable Judge
Rand got to his feet and went after another beer.
"Grenallo admitted to it in his statement."

"Makes me wonder what else he might have been
ready to spill."

Martin Rand looked J.D. straight in the eyes. His
voice grew earnest, his jaw tight with anger. He saw
too much, too well, and he *had* put together the rest.
"Let's drop this little game of ring-around-the-rosie
and get it out on the table, J.D. Are you now suggesting *I* had anything to do with Grenallo killing
himself?"

J.D. believed, with all his heart, that there had to
be someone even more powerful behind John Grenallo. He couldn't help wanting to give Rand the benefit of the doubt. "Did you?"

"No."

"Why don't I believe you, Marty? Why is it I get
the distinct impression you are giving me one last
warning?"

"Because you're in trouble, J.D.," Rand snapped.

"*Deep* trouble. I'm not even the messenger. A hundred to one, you're wearing a bullet-proof vest even now. You know your life isn't worth a plug nickel on the street. Give it up, man! Think! Is this worth it? Haven't you and Weisz and Guiliani done enough? Every one of the TruthSayers you wanted is dead or behind bars."

But Rand's congratulatory spin rang hollow as deadwood rotted from the inside out. J.D.'s heart ached worse than his head. Rand was right about one thing. J.D. saw now that he was mentally and spiritually spent by the weeks on end of holding out against the lies and secrets of coconspirator Truth-Sayers he had believed to be colleagues.

But he had either wandered into some impenetrable thicket of paranoid delusions, or his best friend had been playing J.D. like his coveted Stradivarius for a very, very long time.

BY THE TIME Ann drove home that night, the rain had stopped but the bite of the February cold lingered. She parked in her usual place, beneath the street lamp, and knocked at the front door.

For security reasons, she had made the back door off limits to everyone including herself. She couldn't seal it. With as many as twenty-five women and children under her roof at any given moment, fire regulations demanded another exit.

The sound of Joel's lumbering steps surprised her. Most nights, he was waiting to let her in. This night he had a child, a four-year-old girl named Keely, clinging to his leg, trying awfully hard not to be seen.

Ann understood. Perfectly. Times were, at Keely's age, she hadn't wanted to be seen either. She'd never been spared, always noticed, every infraction, most stray thoughts, though she'd never been beaten like this little one.

Dog-tired, longing for a hot shower, she winked at Keely's mom who sat on a sofa nursing another baby—and at the dim gentle giant who took such good care of the women and kids in Ann's absence.

Joel's IQ wasn't even average, but he scented danger coming a mile away. He stood only five feet five inches, seemed as big around as he was tall and had a sweet face to match his disposition. But Joel understood very well how to lock the house down, when to flip the security switch that would bring him serious help inside of nine minutes.

She plucked a couple of red-licorice ropes from the package in her coat pocket, one for the attached child, the other for Joel. A little hand snaked up and snatched away the treat.

Ann played along while she checked out the fading bruises on Keely's arms and torso. "Now where did that candy get to?"

"What candy would that be, missy Ann?" Joel stalked off, the little girl in her too-short pants and no shirt riding his foot finally giggling. Finally understanding that she wasn't going to be in any trouble this night.

Ann remained downstairs until the last mom had gone to bed, then wandered through the kitchen for a glass of milk. Every industrial-size stainless-steel appliance gleamed, every cafeteria-style table set for breakfast.

When the phone rang at five minutes before midnight, she had undressed to her panties and bra, and only just turned on the water in the tiny corner shower tucked away between her dressing table and a ficus tree. She reversed the spin on the shower knob, made a dash for her bed and snatched the cellular out of her purse.

"Calder."

"Ann… It's—"

Edgy and elusive, a stillness came over her, a flutter of anxiety, tendrils of something almost like shame because she imagined he spoke her single-syllable name like a prayer. "Thorne? J.D.?"

"Yeah." A weariness pervaded his answer, altered, a little, she thought, with pleasure because she'd recognized his voice.

She remembered a night in Wyoming that she'd fallen asleep with her head in his lap. "Where are you?"

"Across the street. In the phone booth."

"On the corner." She held the phone aside and eased back into the sweater dress she'd only just removed. "My corner?"

"See for yourself."

She padded barefoot to windows overlooking the street and pulled aside the lacy homemade curtains. A silvery Cadillac drove slowly by going east, blocking her view, then a black van headed west on the side of the street opposite her house.

J.D. stood leaning against the glassed-in confines of the old-fashioned phone booth under the faux-Hollywood neon klieg lights of the video store, looking up at her. At the curb, illegally parked, sat a lime-green Camaro she'd seen only once before.

Her breath jammed.

On her corner stood the devil in blue jeans and a sheepskin vest. From three stories up and across the street, she could feel his steady brown eyes fixed on her silhouette. Was the slow and shameless smile coming on only in her imagination?

She thought he might not have had a reason to smile in weeks. She didn't begrudge him one, only its genesis if that was her. She had warned him, hadn't she? Warned him against coming around? He had no business on her street corner. "Don't you have a cell phone?"

"I ditched it."

"Why?"

"Didn't want anyone to know where I am. Where I was going." He fell silent for a stretch she let go on to gauge the stress in him. "They only have to ring, you know, to get a fix on location."

She knew. Tracking technology was such a double-edged sword. Privacy was dead. She couldn't even keep things from herself. But whom was he avoiding? "You shouldn't have come here."

"That's what I kept telling myself."

"You promised."

"I know." His smile faded. Foreboding welled up in her. Why now? Why, after all these weeks of keeping his promise, why call her now? She could only think he was half-drunk or in trouble.

She watched him gripping the back of his neck as a teenage couple exited the video store behind him, then a middle-aged woman. A private uniformed security guard went in to make sure the place closed down without any trouble. Overkill, she thought, in her quiet neighborhood.

"Guess I lied," he admitted. "I want to see you, Ann."

How could she make him go when something

greater than simple unruliness urged her to invite him in? Weakness wasn't in her self-definition. "Thorne, it's not a good—"

"Ann—"

"What?"

"Don't. Don't send me away... I need to talk. Things are heating up. I don't know who else I can talk to."

She registered at last the shadows—was it despair?—he tried to keep out of his voice. In the same instant, the uniformed security guard locked up the store and the dark vehicle that had crept by a few moments ago peeled out around the corner.

Her foreboding magnified, then twisted into horror as a rifle shot smashed into the phone booth. Glass erupted in a cloud of shards, blotting J.D. from view for that split second.

She screamed at him through the phone to get down. The security guard coming out of the video store pulled his weapon and dropped to one knee. Shielded by his car, he fired on the black vehicle, then fell heavily. She stepped into her clogs, and took only the time to grab her weapon, then turned and ran, flying downstairs as another shot rang out and then another, then a fourth, she thought from the guard's handgun, before the vehicle roared off and silence fell.

She stumbled into Joel. His eyes bugging out, he blocked the only door. "You don't be going out there, missy Ann. You call for help."

"Joel, it's okay. The shooting has stopped. I need you to go upstairs and get my purse off my dresser. Will you do that, Joel? I need my badge and keys." It took precious seconds before Joel could see his way clear to letting his trust in her override his protective nature, but at last he nodded and moved, and she'd thrown back the dead bolts before he reached the stairs. "Make sure the women and children stay inside."

Her own instincts went into high gear as she slipped out the door. Her sidearm raised, her wrist supported by her other hand, her attention split, focused on danger still lurking and on the security guard swearing a blue streak. She called out to the rent-a-cop, identifying herself as a cop as well, then darted across the street, reaching J.D. first.

She made herself approach him with a professional disregard of her horror, ignore her feelings for him in order to assess his wounds. From shards of glass exploding about him, his head and neck and face and hands oozed blood, but she could see no mortal wounds, no serious gushing.

But a bullet had penetrated his shirt, slamming into his bullet-proof vest at the level of his solar plexus, making his head whiplash into the booth, raising an angry hematoma the size of an egg.

He lay sprawled half into the street, his handsome head tilted at an unnatural angle against the metal frame of the shattered glass booth. Stunned, barely conscious, he was still reaching reflexively for the weapon he hadn't had time to pull.

She replaced the safety on her own gun and put it down, then grabbed his wrist to prevent his reach. He no longer needed his weapon. He could be dangerous if he drew it. She cupped his whiskered, tired, bleeding face in her hands and spoke sharply, as afraid of the exhaustion she saw in his face as she was of saying his name aloud. Even the rent-a-cop could turn out to be one of the killer TruthSayers. "It's over. Just lie still while I think what to do."

She watched him trying to fight through unimaginable pain to clear his head. "Ann?"

"Yes."

"What are you doing here?" His words slurred badly. His overpowering dark brown eyes glittered. "You've gotta get out of here—"

"I know." Tears sprang to her own eyes. He was the one in terrible danger, a man marked by his own kind for death, wounded, bleeding and incoherent, and still *she* was the one he wanted out of harm's way. "I'll get us both out of here—"

"—have to go, have to get the bastards before—"

"I know. I know." She dashed her useless, weakling tears away. She had no plan, nowhere to turn, no haven, only her wits to go on, and her wits felt scattered, blown to kingdom come. "Just *please* don't move for a minute, okay?"

"Hey!" The security guard hollered at her. "I need help. Name's Waltham. I'm down…took a shot in the leg. I musta left my damn radio in the car. I don't think I can get to it."

She begged J.D. to stay put and darted to Waltham's side. She had to think fast now, make no mistakes, find a way to disappear with a wounded, bleeding, marked man without leaving another man dead in their wake.

Joel came rumbling across the street, her purse, cell phone and rolls of gauze cradled in his oversize hands. Anxious to help her, Joel dropped his heavy frame down beside her.

"I'll get an ambulance here," she promised Waltham, ripping open a couple of packets of gauze. She applied them to the pulsing hole in Waltham's leg. "Joel, you hold these, and keep adding more so you don't touch too much blood. And don't let go until the ambulance comes, all right?"

Nodding, Joel focused all his scant attention on what she'd asked him to do. Waltham, however, understood her intentions. "You can't leave the scene of a crime! Hey! You can't do this! Come back here!"

But she was already back to J.D.'s side. She tore open more gauze, and used up a roll of gauze trying to get adequate pressure on the hematoma.

Waltham threw a fit. "Hey! You've gotta call for backup. I need an ambulance. You can't—"

"This man is a protected witness," she hissed over her shoulder, improvising, all but snapping, losing control. "This should never have happened. He's not dangerous, but he slipped his guards. His protection has broken down, and if I don't get him out of here, he'll be dead before morning. Just stay calm and you'll get your damn ambulance."

And please God, she prayed, not caring that she had sworn at him one second and called on God the next. Please don't let him be one of *them*. Don't let him be one of the scheming murderers.

Chapter Three

She tucked the bloodied end of the gauze roll beneath the bandaging job she'd done, then crouched by J.D., angling her body to get one of his arms over her shoulders. "Look at me. You have to get up, Thorne, and you have to do it *right now*. Don't you dare pass out on me. Don't do it!"

But his head lolled back, his eyes stuttered closed. She was going to lose him. With no other choice, she slapped him hard. He came to, staring hard at her, angry because his head hurt and for all he knew, it was her fault. She knew he must hurt so bad he couldn't see straight or hold a thought. She would just have to goad him into moving.

She ducked her head into the shoulder strap of her purse and crammed her handgun inside it, then braced her legs, willing on herself the strength to do what had to be done. She wrapped his right arm tightly around her shoulders and rose, hauling his body up with her on the strength of her thighs.

He was heavy. "Move it, Thorne. *Concentrate.* Stay with me. Stick it out."

She heard Waltham bellowing.

She heard Joel mumbling, wondering what he was

supposed to do, his mental capacities too taxed to enlist his help.

She heard J.D. protesting, anger mixed up like a ball of snakes in his pain as he fought her supporting him. "Ann, you can't do this. They'll—"

"Don't." Anger of her own spewed into her veins. She wouldn't stop, couldn't stop. She had to keep going. Momentum was all she had going for her. "Don't tell me what I can and cannot do, Thorne."

He had nearly a foot on her, but somehow, by some grace, leaning heavily on her, J.D. lost track of trying to spare her or boss her around. He kept his legs beneath him till she crossed the street to her '86 Honda. Angling hard to open the rear door, she managed to maneuver his solidly muscled, crumpling body into the back seat of her car.

From an uncertain distance, the wail of police sirens came at her. One of the women inside must have called the police. At least she wouldn't have to make the call herself. She shoved J.D.'s dangling booted foot hard, slammed the car door, then snatched the keys from the outer pocket of her purse. She had gotten in and only just pulled around the corner and out of sight when the squad cars came screaming in.

From the corner of her eye, she saw J.D. struggling to sit up. "Stay down. We're not out of the woods."

He sank back down and, she thought, passed out. She was not only not out of the woods, she had no idea what to do or where to go.

She turned on her headlights seven blocks away, pulled onto the freeway to blend in with the scant traffic and admitted to herself that she knew without thinking where she could take him.

She knew one place where he would be safe,

where outsiders weren't allowed in and cops had never, ever been needed or welcome. The only problem was that she was not welcome, either, in the rigidly conservative Community of Brethren of Cold Springs, Montana.

She couldn't let that matter.

Cold Springs was several hundred miles away— which promised nothing, considering how widespread and pervasive the TruthSayers had grown to be. But inside the community, they would be safe. No one kept a silence like the brethren.

Tourists were barely tolerated. Violence was anathema, guns unheard of. And though Cold Springs was in the thick of identified TruthSayer vigilantes, no one would come looking for J.D. Thorne in the *Bruderhof,* and no one would go looking for someone to tell, either.

She drove down the interstate for an hour, forcing herself past her own exhaustion to think what she must do. In that time, no sound, save an occasional groan, came from the back seat of the car, but every time she heard him her heart went through another emotional hoop she'd never expected or imagined. Each time, she goaded herself toward what she knew she had to do.

She would have to ditch the Honda. There were places she knew where she could leave it and no one would notice a car so used and beat-up as hers for days. But her chances of making a clean escape would be far better if she could make it look as if she had run in another direction than she intended altogether.

She needed help.

She signaled to move into the right-most lane, then

took the off-ramp, drove beneath the elevated inter-state and got back on, headed in the direction from which she'd just come. No one followed her. J.D. groaned and struggled to get up, but he passed out again from the pain before she could get out a word of warning.

She drove back into the heart of the city on the highway and exited to one of its seediest neighbor-hoods. She had spent her first years on the Seattle police force here, right in the thick of the highest rate of crime in the Pacific Northwest. Here, drug money abounded. The cars trafficking through the neighbor-hood cost more than the buildings, and the high roll-ers supplying the trade ruled.

Her captain had never believed she would make it through that kind of hell, that necessary proving ground.

Her captain proved wrong. He didn't know what she'd been through to get even that far. Once she'd survived it, he made sure she got her shot at the detective bureau.

She was about to sacrifice it all, her entire career. She refused to console herself that the sacrifice wasn't a distinct possibility. J.D. had made powerful enemies of dirty cops and dirtier politicians. There were no more self-righteous or fierce or vindictive men than cops and pols gone over to the other side. They recognized no "other side," only their own.

But she would not abandon the one man still fight-ing for freedoms she held too dear to a fate they had clearly decreed. She would not leave J. D. Thorne to die no matter what it cost her.

She crossed through three intersections, then turned into a back alley unlit by any street lamps.

One building occupied the entire block. She turned in at the chop shop she knew was concealed behind the third set of warehouse garage doors. Dousing the headlights, she turned on the interior ceiling light, rolled down her window and tapped lightly on the horn.

The well-lubricated garage door hummed open. Manny Cordova stood to one side. The Wrecker, they called him on these streets, fifty-seven years old, crippled up and badly scarred, as likely to blow away an unknown intruder as look at one. In the near dark he stood training an AK–47 and a powerful flashlight on her.

Cordova was a dangerous man. She swallowed hard, praying he would recognize her. She called out, "Manny, it's Ann. Ann Calder."

Burns had caused the worst of his scars, from fires erupting in the wake of incendiary bombs meant to wipe him out of business six years ago. Ann had pulled him from the fire, saved his life. He owed her and he knew it, but that didn't make him happy to see her.

He lowered the flashlight and waved her inside.

The garage door closed up behind her. A single lightbulb hung from the ceiling, but it wasn't turned on. The only light came from a Coleman lamp on a torn-up card table in the far corner, where a couple of Manny's cronies sat huddled around a space heater and a bottle of Jack Daniel's.

She counted eleven other vehicles inside the garage besides her own, all in various states of being dismantled and rendered unrecognizable by either the authorities or their previous owners.

She switched off the ignition and got out as Manny lowered his weapon and peered into her car.

"This better not be some trick—"

"It's not." She closed her door. "I wouldn't do that to you, Manny."

"What are you doin' here this time of night, Ann?" He smelled of liquor and pot and she'd bet he hadn't bathed in a month of Sundays. "And who's the stiff in back?"

"I need help, Manny."

"I think I asked you," he said, dragging out his words, "who's the stiff in the back?"

"A friend. He's no concern of yours. You don't have to worry about him. He's unconscious. Will you help me or not?"

"That depends on what you want." Some snickering issued from the pair at the card table. She understood them to be offering another kind of help. Manny swung around and told them to shut the hell up, then turned his back on Ann. "Step into my office."

She realized her own weapon was stuck in the pocket of J.D.'s vest. She knew better than to leave herself this vulnerable, but "excuse me, I just need to get my sidearm first" wasn't an option. There was nothing she could do about it now. She followed Manny Cordova through the garage, past the card table. Both his creepy, leering sidekicks came on her heels through the door to Manny's so-called office.

It only occurred to her then that the worse mistake might have been leaving J.D. alone.

HE REACHED UP to disable the ceiling light, then hooked the door handle with his boot, released the latch and shoved the car door open. The movement nearly cost him all consciousness.

His head pounded. His body felt sluggish, as if he'd been beaten to a pulp. He'd taken a direct hit to his bullet-proof vest, but he couldn't remember what had happened. Only about Ann. He'd been talking to Ann and then… What?

At first he thought he was dreaming, talking to Ann. How else could it have happened? But then, fighting his way up from the unrelenting sea of blackness, his body crammed into the back seat of a car, a stabbing pain in his armpit, bombs bursting in his head, he heard what he thought was her soft voice, dickering with some disrespectful lowlife.

He must be dreaming, except that the door moved when he shoved on it and he almost went under the siege of pain again, so he knew this had to be happening.

But he didn't know what had already happened. He didn't want Ann dickering with thugs. Didn't want… He couldn't think, couldn't reason this out.

He eased himself from the car, inching along the bench seat, letting his body sink to the floor where the scent of grease and filth came at him like an amp of ammonia. He crouched low as if he were in the midst of a war zone, as if he'd been born to one, as if the smoky flare of incoming grenades were real and not just in his head.

Amidst the scatter of auto parts and pieces, of tools and grime and the dark, it finally came to him that this was a chop shop.

Ann, what are you doing? He reached by instinct for the gun in his shoulder holster.

The grip felt sticky. His head swam. He pulled out

his weapon and found his hand smeared with blood. At some primitive level of his mind, he understood this was his own blood, issuing from that stabbing pain beneath his arm. He fought off a surge of bile, the certainty of retching up his guts, forcing himself to abandon cover and follow the sound of an angel's voice.

He came upon the office unseen, absorbing essential details. The glowing space heater aimed at the card table. The remains of joints, too many cigarettes. The bottle of Jack Daniel's, three-quarters empty. Three shot glasses. He leaned into the wall so he wouldn't have to give in to falling on his knees.

Three of them. One of him.

He focused as hard as he could, what with the war zone in his head, on what was going down on the other side of the wallboard.

"We're not working any deal till I get a clear picture of who's the stiff in your junker, sweet Annie. Stiffs an' me in the same context, ya know, don't go over."

"Manny, I told you. Who he is is nothing to you. He's not dead, only hurt. Badly. I need a truck or station wagon," he heard the angel's voice dealing with the devil.

Ann, he thought, recognizing himself for the stiff in question. *What are you doing?*

"There was a tan and white pickup out there," he heard Ann continue. "That one would do."

"Too bad. I'm looking to keep that'n for myself."

It came to J.D., as it must, as out of the years he had spent dealing with the lowlife's kind, that it wouldn't have mattered which vehicle she picked out. That would be the one the creep wanted for himself. Beyond that, J.D. couldn't think, couldn't remember, had not the foggiest clue what she was doing, save dealing with the devil, and doing it on his behalf.

He couldn't remember what had happened, didn't *know.*

Ann's voice: "You can have it back when I'm done."

A pause. The pause of a beady-eyed slug seeing the deal wasn't going to cost him as much as he'd thought at first. "Is that all?"

"No. I need Montana plates. And someone to drive my car down the coast."

"No way I've got clean plates."

"Not even—"

"No. Not even." Chop shops didn't deal in unfettered license plates.

"I can maybe get one of these clowns to take a Sunday drive with your car—" more snickering "—but the truck and plates are out, sweetheart."

The disrespect hit J.D. all wrong, like a sucker punch. He felt himself begin to shake. His fists tightened, one around his sticky gun grip, the other on itself. He forced himself past the pain in his head to examine what he could remember before he did something stupid. More stupid.

He'd been caught unaware, unprepared.

He'd let himself be shot full in the chest, taken down, out of action.

And somehow he'd put Ann in the position of begging for a way to get him out of danger—danger he'd put her in as well. Nausea swept through him again like a wave of sewage, half pain-induced, half at the realization that he had dragged Ann Calder into his nightmare.

He'd wanted to see her, be with her. He remembered that. But not like this. He had to get out of here, out of harm's way till his head didn't hurt so damn bad. Till his mind cleared and he could think again.

He could go to ground. He'd been there, done that. Learned to take cover at his uncle Jess's knee. His armpit felt on fire, his chest hollowed. His head bobbled, threatening to drop off his shoulders, but he swore to himself he could get out of here and get into hiding without dragging Ann down with him.

She had to be cut out of his waking nightmare and it had to happen now, before she got in any deeper. Before she became a target right alongside him.

Hell wouldn't have J. D. Thorne if something happened to her on his account.

Through the rockets flaring in his head, through the wallboard, he heard her steely insistence, Manny's reluctant agreement, the deal arranged. Bodies shuffled, a chair scraped. He breathed in and out, felt the adrenaline surge rising up. He backed up tight against the wall, gun in his left hand, raised to his shoulder.

He thought he was feeling no pain. He thought he'd pull this off.

Manny came out the door, turning into the warehouse garage, still bellyaching, followed by Ann. J.D. let the second lowlife cross the threshold before he brought the butt of his gun down hard over his head, then got a chokehold on the head of the third guy. The punk stiffened with fear, unwittingly turning himself into the crutch that kept J.D. standing upright when the pain erupted from beneath his arm and poured like molten lava through his whole body.

Still he trained his gun with deadly accuracy on Manny, who had turned on Ann, shrieking in rage. J.D. fired at the filthy concrete floor just behind Manny. The bullet ricocheted harmlessly away. The blast had its intended effect.

Manny froze, his scarred, anvil-shaped face a mask of hate. Ann had ducked behind the fender of the tan and white pickup. He could see her ashen face, knew she couldn't believe he had even regained consciousness. He saw the worry. He was as dangerously unpredictable as a gut-shot grizzly.

He readjusted his chokehold on Manny's thug friend. Bludgeoned so nearly senseless by pain, he had no feel for subtlety. Still he tried to infuse an explanation into the utter dismissal he barked at her, as if he had been in charge and using her to broker this penny-ante deal all along. "Get lost, babe. I'll take it from here."

She stood, slowly. "Don't be an idiot! You can't—"

"I can do anything I want," he snarled, his eyes warning her not to give him away. "You're out, you see?"

"What kind of crapola is this?" Equally wary of J.D., Manny spat epithets at her. "You said this was no trick."

"She lied," J.D. snapped. "She didn't want to die tonight, see, so she shut her mouth and did what she was told."

This was the account of the night J.D. wanted to impress on his unwilling host, so that when the cops came around, as they would, in droves, it would be understood by one and all that Ann Calder had been his hostage, not his rescuer. He knew of no other way to absolve her, to protect her.

His pain grew so rigid and unbending that he didn't know if he could walk, let alone drive, but he saw through the haze that she understood his intent.

That she felt betrayed.

Furious.

If looks could kill, she would have finished the job then and there, but they couldn't, and that was the point. Let her live with her fury.

At least she would be alive to live it.

He had to get this over. He ordered the outraged Manny into the trunk of a car the man had been in the process of relieving of its sound system, then hobbled along on the back of the scared-stiff punk still in his chokehold, ordering him to close the trunk. When J.D. reached the pickup, he let the wiry punk go with a warning to run and a threat of a bullet in the back if he stopped. The guy bolted for the door beside the larger automatic garage door and disappeared.

Then J.D. had only Ann left to confront. He clung to the heavy-duty side mirror on the pickup to forestall falling on his face and sent her a look meant to forestall her interference. She had an advantage over Manny and his thugs.

She knew he wouldn't shoot her.

She began to walk toward him. The fire in her eyes turned their gray a molten silver, but her voice was sweet as a choir of angels. "J.D., you will fall asleep at the wheel. Please don't do this."

The nearer she got, the weaker he felt, Samson to her Delilah.

"I couldn't let it happen—"

"Couldn't be rescued by a woman, you mean?"

He snarled at her. "That's asinine."

"Oh. Then you're saving me from myself? Is that it?"

Pretty much. His heart pounded; he felt its effects in the spurt of fresh warm blood spilling down his side. He had preempted her, run afoul of her in so fundamental a way that to protect her values she was willing to stand here watching him bleed to death.

"Stay away, Ann," he said through clenched teeth. "It's done."

"No. It's not done. All you've done is prove—" Her voice broke. She swallowed and balled up her fists. "You're incompetent to save even yourself right now."

She kept coming closer. He felt vaguely threatened, then thought he must be confused. She represented no threat to him. Still he didn't trust her or the situation. "Don't come any closer."

His warning missed its mark.

She swallowed. Tears glittered in her eyes. Sweetness and light replaced the steeliness, throwing him another curve. "You're losing a lot of blood. You're *hurt,* J.D. Don't do this. You can't last. You won't make it alone."

"I will." Confusion rankled about in his head. "Just get out of my w—" But the arm he had wrapped around the sideview mirror gave out and she moved in, using her body to hold him up against the door of the pickup.

Waves of blackness were a heartbeat from taking him under, yet he saw her delicate, finely honed features with a surreal clarity. Her forehead, those stoppingly beautiful streetwise eyes, the fringe of her lashes, a handful of freckles.

The anger etched in each tiny line on her lips.

He frowned. That wasn't what he wanted at all. How had this all gotten so out of hand?

Someone had tried to kill him. How in the hell had he let it happen?

"Ann," he uttered thickly. "Let me go."

But she anchored her body more firmly against his, took hold of the sheepskin lapels of his vest and let herself inside, molding her body to his. "Take me."

Take me. Other connotations swam in his head. Such a terrible irony.

Distantly, he heard the thug Manny kicking and bellowing to be let out of the trunk. The cold cavernous garage shrank till all J.D. knew was Ann, till the softness of her breasts against him made all the pain recede to nothing, till her lips grazed his jaw and her sweet hot trembling tongue touched his neck.

His poor head reeled. Her heat invaded him. Drugged him.

Seduced him.

Against all odds, he grew hard and his head grew lighter still and he finally understood that had been her intent. The oldest trick in the book.

He would have laughed if he'd been able to stay conscious another few seconds. Or if he weren't in the worst straits of his life, taking her down with him.

Chapter Four

By eleven-thirty the next morning Ann had reached
the turnoff twenty miles outside the town of Cold
Springs to the home she had abandoned fifteen years
before.

She'd had to deal with Manny, but she had always
kept five hundred dollars stashed behind the radio in
her car. She'd given it to him, along with her credit
card to buy gas for the Honda to take it south. He
could only do so much damage with the thousand
dollars left on her card.

Her cell-phone battery had gone dead, so she'd
been forced to take the time to stop at a pay phone
still inside Seattle to leave a message on the machine
at Social Services. Her message said only that she
had been called out of town. Someone would be assigned to oversee the day-to-day operations of the
halfway house.

In Missoula, she'd stopped to buy gasoline, douse
J.D.'s wound with a bottle of liquor from a drive-
through and pack a wad of napkins into the armhole
of his bullet-proof vest.

Still, the drive across I–90, through the mountains
to I–15 and then north, had taken her eleven hours.

She couldn't imagine a worse time to arrive than the middle of the day. All the adult eyes and ears of the colony would be gathered together for the midday meal.

Let the humbling of Annie Tschetter begin.

The farm sat nestled in the foothills of the Rockies. Snow blanketed all but the trodden paths between the ten or twelve buildings, the longhouses, four of them, aligned perfectly north to south and each divided into four apartments, the community kitchen, the live-stock pens and cattle barns, the school, the book-binder's hut and machine shop and preacher's quarters.

In all the years she'd been gone, nothing essential changed here. The place was what it was, a bastion against a sin-filled world.

She felt a powerful familiarity that choked her, a fear of going back almost too sharp to bear. She had to be stronger than that. Slouched and unconscious against the passenger door, J.D. depended on it.

She shoved in the clutch and downshifted as she made the final turn and pulled into the yard halfway between the preacher's workplace and the dining hall.

Before she could lose her nerve, she jumped down out of the pickup and trudged across the hard snow in her clogs and climbed the stairs. She knocked on the door of the preacher, who took his midday meal alone so his work and contemplation would not be disturbed.

A large, snowy-white napkin tucked by a corner into his collar, Micah Wilmes opened the door, most unhappy to be disturbed, he wanted it understood from the outset.

"What is it?"

She told herself she knocked at the doors of unhappy people every day of her life. He was no different. But as he stood there staring at her from his narrowed eyes, she knew he *was* different. Along with the five who governed life here, he held in his hands the power to grant her asylum for J.D., or to turn her away.

She had believed he would know her by her hair alone, but he showed no sign whatsoever of recognition. "Elder, it's Annie Tschetter." Calder was the name she used in the outside world. "Tschetter" fell from her lips as naturally as if she'd used it every day of her life, too. "I need your help. I need shelter for a wounded man—"

"Gott im Himmel!" He recoiled a bit as utter disbelief seized his narrow, harsh features. What she had done all those years ago had never been done. He hadn't known how to deal with her then, or before, any more than he knew how to deal with her brazen return. "You dare—"

But he clamped his jaw shut, jerked the napkin from his collar and hurtled past her down the unadorned wooden steps to his quarters. He turned back and pointed a bony finger at her, commanding her in the German dialect as if ordering the devil behind him. *"Get off my steps!"*

Wilmes had not crossed the square to the kitchen and dining hall before men in black jeans and heavy coats and fearsome beards quietly got up from their dinner plates to deal with an outsider who dared disturb the peace and reflection of the minister.

The women and children would be expected to keep themselves apart from this, but from the school,

Ann saw faces crowding at the windows to see what was the commotion.

Almost by osmosis, every woman and child would learn that the wild, wanton, unrepentant youngest daughter of Hannah and Peter Tschetter had returned, begging unheard-of favors from the community she had first shamed and then spurned.

The men of the faithful, baptized and as yet unbaptized, parted like the sea before Moses, giving the colony manager wide berth.

Ann recognized more than half of the men. Many of their names refused to come to her. Not his. Twenty-one years her senior, the colony manager was her own brother.

Timothy.

Saying nothing, his features harder than granite, he halted ten feet from her. Wilmes stood at his side, forming a united front.

"I need sanctuary for a wounded man." She called out to make herself heard over the keening wind, thinking only yesterday she had been reminded in court that she had faced sterner stuff than Morton Downey.

Before her now stood her brother, old enough to be her father, solid, tall, his dark beard graying, his dark eyes unrelenting. He was the man to whom she had run every time her hands were strapped or she was shut away or brought before the German teacher or the preacher. Of all her other brothers—Jakob, Johannes, Martin, Andreas and Georg—who now stood behind him, only Timothy had come close to understanding her.

But after all these years, Timothy was himself transformed into the sterner stuff of the colony boss, and for a moment she lost all heart. She couldn't remember how she had ever had the courage or the sheer willful stamina to defy them at all. To defy a kind of socialization that brooked no semblance of a self.

Timothy crossed his arms. "Your hair is loose."

His indictment condensed into a single statement the catalog of her sins. She was a woman, therefore weaker and in need of guidance, emotional, spiritual, intellectual.

She had no business out in the world alone, no business dragging her obscene and worldly problems here, no respect for herself or them with her headstrong and wanton ways. Her hair, caught in the wind, announced all that to these men.

But then her hair had marked her for a troublemaker the first hour out of her mother's womb. The pain splintered through her as if it were fresh, and not so very old and trite. If her hair had been brown, she thought. If her mother hadn't died bringing her into the world. If she had been ordinary, if she hadn't been regarded and thus treated as a devil seed. Would she have turned out differently then? Would she have sacrificed herself before she even knew what she was giving up? Would she have stayed here and married Samuel?

She caught up her wind-tossed hair and held it bunched at her nape. "I meant no disrespect, Timothy."

His eyes traveled her body. Catching up her hair made her posture immodest, and she knew the bitter cold wind, slicing through her, plastered the soft burgundy mohair sweater dress to her legs and breasts. "You reek of disrespect."

She let go her hair and gritted her teeth. "The man in the pickup is badly injured. Will you give us asylum?"

"Does the faithful knowingly give the devil purchase?" Wilmes demanded. Ever the hawk on the Lord's behalf. There was no room for mercy in the stern heart of the Reverend Wilmes, but she could not get into it with him. Not now. Not ever.

She heard a few murmurs of assent, or imagined them coming from men nodding their heads in agreement with Wilmes, and then she saw Samuel behind Andreas and Georg. Among all the bearded men, he stood out, clean-shaven.

Her throat locked tight. Samuel had never married, for if he had, he would wear a beard as well. But a man over forty might as well, married or not, so his shaving was a statement he made every day of his life. He had been humiliated by Annie Tschetter, and no one would forget that till he took his bare face to his grave.

She had asked for asylum. Everyone knew the preacher's opinion. She waited on her brother's reply.

"Take him to the hospital," he pronounced at last and turned away, as if to return to his meal and wipe from the slate of this day her ungodly interruption.

"I can't do that, Timothy," she called out.

Her brother turned back around, clearly not quite believing even she would persist when she had clearly been given her answer. "Why?"

"His wounds are from bullets. At a hospital, all gunshot injuries are reported to the police. If that happens, he will be found, and they will not fail again to kill him."

The gathered men began to mutter among themselves. "What *they* is this?" her brother mocked her. She could hear as if it were yesterday her teacher's constant admonitions. *You are either in the Ark, Annie Tschetter, or you are not.*

To Timothy, to all the colony, *they* was a generic term for anyone outside the Ark, all the godless, evil men who ran amok with their guns, killing each other, spreading death and destruction like weeds. "Enlighten me, please," he commanded. "What *they* do you mean?"

She was ready for this, but not so prepared for sarcasm. "Men just like the ones who burned out your silos and your barns last fall, Timothy. Men just like them. They call themselves the TruthSayers."

The name caused a vague stir of recognition among the men.

She had seen in the news more than a year ago that the Community of Brethren outside Cold Springs, Montana, had contracted to buy another eight thousand acres, enough land to support a daughter colony forty miles to the south. Cold Springs had been only a year old when Ann ran away, with sixty-eight people in twelve families. By now there would be more than the one hundred and fifty or so that made necessary a division of the colony.

Whether TruthSayers had committed the arson or not, she knew she had struck a powerful chord. There was no difference in the mentality of TruthSayers and those who destroyed the harvest of the colony. The sale had fallen through when the harvest and collateral dollars were no longer there.

Now she knew by the angered expressions. Even

in their separate world, these men knew and feared the persecution from the TruthSayers.

"Get back in your truck and leave this place. We are not for you," Timothy said.

She felt his words land like blows to the body. He could not be clearer. "He will die, Timothy. Without your help—" She cut her plea short. At least he hadn't turned away. "Not everyone on the outside is evil, Timothy. Some of us are struggling—"

"Who is the man in the truck?" he demanded sharply, cutting her off, unwilling to hear anything about *some of us*. "What is he to you?"

"My husband." The lie spilled from her lips before she knew what she would say, a desperate lie offered up in some futile notion that it would make a difference to Timothy that she had done what she had sworn never to do. That she had taken a husband. That it might turn the tide of rejection before it became carved in stone. "He's a good and decent man, Timothy. An honorable man," she pleaded, "who's fighting against the TruthSayers and everything they stand for."

The preacher scoffed. A man was a fool to believe the godless nature of unbelievers could be corrected, a lamb bleating at the sun and the stars to alter their paths through the skies.

For the first time, she considered that she might fail even in the wake of her desperate lie, but as she searched her mind for alternatives, the pickup door creaked open and J.D. fell heavily to the snow-covered ground and fresh blood began to stain the snow a brilliant red.

Confronted with the reality of a bleeding and unconscious man, the good pastor Wilmes and her brother consented to give them refuge.

When she asked them to replace the Washington license plates, she thought he would turn away and send her packing.

He pointed at her instead and laid down his law. "You will see no one, speak to no one. Your meals will be delivered to you. You will be given proper clothing.

"And you will cover your head."

J.D. WAS CARRIED by five men to the back of the bookbinder's hut and laid upon a birthing sheet spread over the large double bed usually given visitors from other colonies. First-aid supplies were delivered along with a cauldron of boiling water carried into the hut by a couple of strong teenage boys who then turned on the gas heater and cracked a window.

Among the women, only the midwife was sent to assist Ann through the crisis of a fresh bleed, and though J.D. reeked of the whiskey Ann had poured onto his wound at the rest stop in the middle of the night, the woman didn't so much as twitch her nostrils. But she didn't speak to Ann, either, except to give her orders.

Ann managed to roll J.D.'s body enough to one side, then the other, to get him out of his sheepskin vest. His gray flannel shirt was another story, glued with his blood to his bullet-proof vest, which was in turn stuck to a T-shirt and his flesh below that.

What Ann saw when the blood and vest and layers had been stripped away made her stomach heave violently. At the instant she had observed him raising his arm to ease the knots in his neck in that phone

booth, a bullet had smashed into the armhole of the
bullet-proof vest and then tumbled, misshapen, tearing a gash in his flesh and lodging in the unprotected
muscles of his armpit.

The midwife sucked air through her teeth as she
bent to the task of plucking the bullet out with a
metal forceps.

The bleeding began again. Swallowing hard, Ann
climbed onto the bed beside him and held pressure
to the artery above his wound while the midwife dis-
infected and stitched together the ragged edges of
J.D.'s fevered flesh.

MATT GUILIANI RUBBED his bleary eyes and got up
for a cup of coffee. He'd been at it all night, closing
in on the end. He'd spent the last twelve weeks plow-
ing through stacks of file folders, reams of paper,
appointment books, calendars, inter- and intra-office
memos and the home computer of the former assistant U.S. attorney John Grenallo. Before that, three
weeks combing through hard copy of every text and
graphic file from the computers in the offices of
Grenallo's secretary, Tess Arubio, and his two top
aides.

He'd done it alone, convinced with solid reason
and the agreement of Grenallo's replacement that,
except for Matt himself, there was no one who could
be completely trusted.

He worked in a near-virtual vault. No windows,
one entry, round-the-clock video security, high-tech
locks on the door. He was beginning to feel like a
mole.

Then, yesterday, he saw the report on the 6:00 a.m.
news while he pumped iron in the fitness complex a

block from his office. J.D. Thorne had been the apparent victim of a drive-by shooting.

Matt had lowered the two-hundred-pound weights on the bench press, sat up and stared hard at the live video feed originating at the scene of the crime. He recognized the video store on the corner across the street from Ann Calder's halfway house. J.D.'s lime-green Camaro was still parked illegally at a fire hydrant. The reporter had done her work and unearthed the name of the proprietor of the halfway house, and from there to the proposition that the woman who had spirited Thorne away, apparently still alive, was in fact Detective Ann Calder. An off-duty police officer, Darrel Waltham, moonlighting for a security company, had been a witness.

The shattered remains of the telephone booth behind the reporter sent a nasty chill up Matt's spine.

He grabbed a towel and headed to the showers. When he reached his office half an hour later, he worked his way from the Department of Justice computers into the Seattle P.D. He didn't even have to hack in. He knew his way around, and he'd been given carte blanche in his solo investigation of Grenallo's affairs to go where his nose took him. He headed straight for the eyewitness report.

All he learned beyond what had been reported was that Waltham claimed to have returned fire but was himself hit. He failed to get a plate number. He didn't know the extent of the injuries to the guy in the phone booth, only that Calder had told Waltham that the victim was a protected witness she had no choice but to remove from the scene and take into hiding. Waltham only learned afterward that the victim was J.D. Thorne.

Matt appreciated instantly Ann's dilemma. For all she knew, the guard was in on the attempt on J.D.'s life, in place to make himself look righteous, or if the shooters in the SUV missed, to make the hit good. She'd improvised brilliantly, gotten J.D. to his feet and into her car—Waltham got that plate number—then disappeared into the night.

Her car had not been found. No gunshot victims had been reported by any physician or hospital emergency room within five hundred miles.

Matt drew a deep breath, pulled a cedar toothpick from his breast pocket, stuck it in his mouth and leaned back in his chair. He had to assume that Ann had weighed the risk of taking J.D. for treatment, thus exposing his whereabouts to the would-be assassins, against getting him to safety and dealing with J.D.'s wounds herself.

Matt couldn't imagine where she'd gone, but he trusted her instincts and her resourcefulness. He'd seen her in action. And he'd seen her looking at J.D. as if he were God's gift to womankind.

Still, his nerves hummed, and it wasn't a pleasant tune.

J.D. must finally have cut too close to the quick in his ongoing investigation of the TruthSayers penetration into legitimate law enforcement. He would have to die. Wherever he was, wherever Ann had taken him, probably wasn't going to be good enough. The bastards were everywhere.

He had exited the Seattle P.D. computers, prepared to get back to his own work, when his pager went off. He pulled the thing off his belt and looked at the digital display at a number he didn't recognize. Times like this, he was annoyed by his own decision not to have an assigned phone number with caller ID. He jabbed the button for a generic line out from the hundred and fifty delegated to the DOJ and then the number on the pager.

"Hello?"

"This is Guiliani. Someone at this number paged—"

"Matt, yes. This is Martin Rand."

U.S. federal judge Martin Rand? Interesting. Matt said nothing.

"J.D.'s friend?" Rand supplied, his intonation asking if Matt now recognized the name. He knew J.D. and Rand knew each other, but played it as if he hadn't a clue. Better to get one than give one away.

"Sorry. I don't—"

"We grew up together. I thought he might have mentioned me."

"Oh yeah, sure. Sorry." He wasn't. Telluride came instantly to his mind, and with it, the nagging notion that the Colorado town had appeared somewhere in the vast quantities of documents he'd been through in the weeks behind him. "Telluride, right?"

"Exactly." Rand paused. "Listen, I know you and J.D. are close, and I'm worried about him."

"The shooting."

"Yes. It's like a nightmare. I told him. I tried to warn him this would happen—"

"When would that have been?" Matt asked.

"He came by my place yesterday afternoon."

"So, you were the last one to see him."

"I doubt it. He left around five. The shooting, as I understand it, didn't take place until midnight or thereabouts. I have no idea where he might have gone after he left, but—'' Rand broke off. ''Can I be frank with you?''

Matt took the toothpick out of his mouth and let his chair spring forward, his internal b.s. detector on full alert. ''Sure. Go ahead.''

''This is...difficult. J.D. and I go way back. But I want to help him and you don't get that accomplished turning a blind eye.'' He went on when Matt said nothing. ''I think he was stretched too thin. I think the stress was getting to him. Frankly, I don't think he was thinking straight even when he was here, and I'm concerned—''

''What would make you think that?''

''He asked me if I had anything to do with John Grenallo's suicide. That's not reflective of the thinking of a man in his rational mind—certainly not J.D.''

Matt sank ever so slowly back in his chair, blown away by J.D.'s instincts. It had been reported in the press that Grenallo had hanged himself before he could be taken into custody—both to avoid prosecution and to spare his family the ordeal. The news reports had faithfully, to the letter, reported the autopsy results as signed out by the medical examiner.

The report was a complete fabrication, but that fact was known only to three people—the medical examiner, Grenallo's replacement, Vince Boyd, and Matt. Grenallo had died of anaphylactic shock—an overblown allergic reaction, and *then* strung up in his own garage, roughly an hour before he had agreed to be taken into custody.

Someone had laced his food with an unknown but extremely powerful allergen.

For J.D. to have posed that question to Martin

Rand told Matt that J.D. suspected that at the very least, Grenallo had hanged himself under duress.

Someone had needed to make sure John Grenallo never talked.

So this, Matt thought, was where J.D. had cut too close to the quick. Whoever had murdered Grenallo had reason now to know that J.D. was closing in on the truth.

As far as Matt knew, however, Martin Rand was clean. His name had never come up in any connection or context even remotely tying him to Grenallo or any other known or suspected TruthSayers. What Matt couldn't guess was whether J.D. had arrived at the truth through sources, or whether it was a brilliant guess. Or how many other places than with Rand J.D. might have floated the possibility of murder.

Matt knew he had to play this with extreme care. He'd been silent too long. His only gambit now was to wait until Rand grew irritated. It didn't take long.

"Are you there?"

"Yeah. Trying to guess where J.D. came up with a theory like that. He's nobody's fool."

"My point exactly."

"Just to be clear, what was your answer?"

"That's offensive, Guiliani," Rand railed. "I am a federal district court judge and—"

"I know that, sir. John Grenallo was one of the most highly placed attorneys in the DOJ, but he was in up to his eyeballs."

"Point taken," Rand snapped, "but the point now is to find J.D. He's not thinking clearly." Matt thought there was nothing wrong with J.D.'s thinking if he had figured out that Grenallo's death was no suicide, but he let Rand go on. "Even if he's not seriously wounded, he could walk into an ambush. If you know where he is, I can get U.S. marshals to him inside of an hour.''

''I don't know where he is.''

''No idea where he might run? Where Calder would head?''

''None.'' And if he had, Matt thought, at this point, the Honorable Judge Martin Rand had hit the top of the list of Matt's least likely confidants.

By noon he'd found the reason why Telluride had stuck in his memory, only to pop up when Rand mentioned the town to establish his long-standing friendship with J.D. Another connection to J.D. and Martin Rand, a rancher from Wyoming, originally Telluride, Colorado, named Kyle Everly. The guy's name had appeared in an appointment book kept for Grenallo by his secretary. The appointment had apparently been scratched, but that alone did nothing to dampen Matt's interest.

Driving home that night, Matt faced the fact that there was nothing he could do to help J.D., nor anything he could personally do to check out the Honorable Judge Rand without sending up alarms.

Garrett, on the other hand, might be able to scare up some relevant details. And in any case, J.D. knew how to get hold of either of them if he really needed help.

It crossed his mind that J.D. might be too severely injured to think of using the credit-card ruse they'd devised as a sort of SOS flare, but by the time he thought of that, Matt discovered that he had picked up a tail.

He wasn't amused.

He toyed with the guy, turning here and there to

confirm his suspicion. In the end, he let himself be followed. He really didn't know where J.D. was.

He would bore his inept tail to death.

And as far as Matt was concerned, Thorne couldn't be in better hands that Ann's. Cupid, he thought, worked in wondrous and terrifying ways.

Chapter Five

J.D. floated in and out of consciousness for what must have been days. The sun set, the sun rose, a bell tolled in the semidarkness. Hours passed. He had the sense of time sifting through his fingers while he wasted his life in a feather bed in another time and place.

Another century.

From the frosted window he saw pioneer children, girls in dark coats over long, dark dresses and white-dotted kerchiefs, boys in black pants and shoes and hats, trekking each morning to a little brick school-house, each afternoon back. He dreamed that it was to dormitories that they returned, but it made no sense, didn't fit.

Nothing made sense to him in his dreamworld in any case. He was fevered, sick, hallucinating the flame-haired woman lying next to him on the feather bed, bending over him, sitting next to him, spooning soup and porridge into him, bathing him with a cloth dipped in a ceramic basin filled with steaming water out of a heavy iron kettle...bathing herself in the flickering light of a gas lantern turned low.

Ann.

He might be hallucinating, but nothing he had seen in all his life came half so close to erotic as the naked contours of her back, or the shape of her full breasts in the shadows on the wall.

Even in the light of day, even in his half-conscious delirium, he could not look at that whitewashed, starkly unadorned wall and not see those images, so he would have to let his half-mast eyelids fall shut to think, in his few lucid moments, what he was doing here.

Snatches of visceral memory dogged him. The sound of glass exploding all around him, a hailstorm of surprise, the sensation of his chest meeting up with a battering ram. Tears glittering, spilling on him. Her voice. Ann's voice. The scent of axle grease and whiskey.

Even the clash of wills with Ann over what was to be done next.

He ranged about in his mind and knew an attack on his life was not unexpected, that he had been warned. It was the nature of the warning that eluded him. He knew who he was, what he had done, the power of the enemies he had made, the truth about too many self-righteous men, but not that.

Not when or how or by whom he had been warned. Not how he should have known the attack was imminent.

Each time he fell into unconsciousness again, he told himself when he woke that he would remember, but each time he drifted up from the black depths, he came this far toward an answer but no further.

It happened again now. He let himself drift off after the small storm of white-dotted scarves disappeared into the school building, and when he awoke again, a powerfully built, fully bearded man in dark work clothes and suspenders sat silently against the whitewashed wall, his powerful arms crossed over his chest, watching J.D.

Seated silent and demurely to his side, Ann was clad in a dark plaid dress with white cuffs and collar, and a dotted kerchief like he'd seen on the little girls. *Why would she want to do that?*

His head felt as thick and muddled as the porridge she had fed him, his arm as if he were hanging from a barbed-wire fence, his chest, sucker-punched over and over again.

Still, he planted his hands on the feather bed and shoved himself up so he could rest his head against the wall behind him. His chest was bare except for the bandaging that stretched like a too-small sling from the far side of his neck, under his arm and around his shoulder blade. That and the bruise.

He realized that he didn't know where his sidearm was.

The bearded man had Ann's eyes. "I've come to take the measure of the man to whom Annie Tschetter would submit herself."

Annie? Tschetter? Submit herself? His mind worked so slowly it took J.D. long moments before a gap cracked open and let in the light. Bewildered, even shocked on so many levels he didn't know where to begin, he looked to Ann. *Something you need to tell me, Annie Tschetter?*

She met his gaze straight on. "J. D. Thorne, this is my brother, Timothy, the colony manager."

As explanations went, this one left him in the dark, but he had not survived ten years undercover by exposing his ignorance. Still, he could count on the fingers of one hand the times he had been so ignorant as this.

What colony was this? Who lived in colonies?

"She's told you about us?" Timothy's words and his demeanor utterly excluded his sister.

J.D. scratched his days-old beard. His head spun. Sometimes he could hardly draw breath. "I'm sorry. Where I was raised, it's impolite to talk about a woman as if she weren't in the room."

"Where would that be?"

"Colorado."

"Home of the unsinkable Molly Brown," Timothy said.

J.D. felt more than saw Ann's surprise at the remark. He only nodded.

"Here, a woman knows her place."

"In the…colony, you mean?"

"Yes."

J.D. shrugged. "*There,* a woman is more than a stick of furniture."

Timothy straightened, challenging, "Is that the picture she gave you of our womenfolk?"

J.D. turned his head slowly from side to side. He felt his focus tightening. "That's the picture you're giving me, Timothy. You're treating your sister as if she weren't even here."

Timothy cleared his throat, dismissing out of hand an untutored, unsolicited opinion. "She says you are a good and decent man. An honorable man."

He felt almost blindsided. What was there to say? Yeah, that's me?

"She says you are hunted. That you have made many enemies among the TruthSayers."

"That's true."

Timothy nodded, forced, obviously, to conclude that J.D. was not of that heinous ilk. "Then what I have to ask is whether or not you believe the colony is in danger for having given you refuge."

It occurred to J.D. at last why Ann had wanted the tan and white pickup. He had seen only utility vehicles out the window of this room. Any passenger car would have been sorely out of place. She'd taken that precaution. "Ann wouldn't do anything to endanger you. I'm sure she's already told you what—"

Ann interrupted him softly. "Timothy's concerns are not assuaged by the judgment of a woman."

Her brother's bull neck reddened. "These are dangerous men. This is a serious matter."

"Not fit for a woman, you mean?" she asked.

"As God is my witness, I say *no*. This is not a fit subject for a woman," he retorted. "This is not a fit subject for man or beast, either! I don't understand you! You had to go, fine. Not one day has passed since you ran away that I have not said to myself, *she had to go.*

"Here you were a caged bird, I said to myself, though the cage was the cross you were given to bear. Here you were dying, I said to myself, all the while thinking you would be better off in the arms of our Heavenly Father than out in the world where such violence as this—" he flung his arm in J.D.'s direction "—is done to a good and honorable man."

He struggled to rein in his outburst. His voice went low and guttural. "If you ask me, Annie Tschetter, is this fitting and proper for a woman, I say no. But not only a woman. This is not a matter fit for savages or mad dogs."

A long silence fell. Ann said nothing, only the

barest tremor of her chin gave away her feelings. J.D. clutched the bandaging over his chest as the gap cracked open a little wider, letting in a little more light. Through the red, blinding haze in his head, he began ever so belatedly to string a few cogent details together.

You live in a three-story building you own and operate as a halfway house for battered women and—runaway children, yes.

Almost…communally. Could we agree on that?

Yes, Mr. Downey, we could agree upon that.

With a shared kitchen and living area?

Yes.

Ann had run away from this place, this…colony, then re-created it in her own way with the halfway house for women and children, a place where men were not allowed. Fleetingly, he thought how devastatingly lonely it must be to live alone in a city like Seattle when you had been brought up in a place like this. He couldn't imagine what had possessed her to return here with him when she must have known what welcome awaited her.

Or to lie to her brother, implying in some way that she had submitted herself to J.D.

Or why she sat there so stoically, making no attempt to answer.

He wouldn't second-guess her, but he didn't know where he fit in all of this, whether he should defend her or if that would only make it all that much worse for her.

Timothy drew himself up and lodged his eyes on his large callused hands, finally throwing down his gauntlet to J.D. "Are you a man who believes a woman belongs in such a world as you inhabit?"

One yardstick, J.D. thought, of his measure as a man. He felt the force of Ann's attention to what he would say. In his heart of hearts, he knew his actions in that chop shop spoke louder to Ann than any answer he offered her brother. His first and last conscious thoughts had been to keep Ann out of danger. How could he answer otherwise?

His pulse throbbed mercilessly in the knot on his head. He didn't even know what he would say when he opened his mouth. "You're asking me if Ann wouldn't be better off dead than alive, living in my world. I don't believe that." But he could see that his answer meant nothing to Timothy, for Ann may be dead to this life, but she would be reaping her eternal rewards in heaven.

J.D. knew nothing of heaven, whether he would get there or whether he wouldn't, only what it took to make his world work. "Do you think your safety here, your privacy, your right to live as you choose, do you believe that comes without a price tag?"

"We take care of our own. We ask nothing—"

"You do, Timothy," Ann contradicted him, speaking up at last. "You ask to be left alone. You demand to be left alone."

"What is that to *them?*" he demanded. "Or to you?"

"Would you be left alone and in peace if it weren't for laws and the people who enforce them? Shall I recite our history? How many times did we flee persecution? How many times to avoid compulsory military service? How many times were our homes burned out and the faithful hounded to death? Isn't that why we're here in America?"

Timothy delivered a terrible scowl intended to

quell the impudence of her giving him a history lesson, but her brother's ironclad opposition seemed only to fuel her outburst. "You get down on your knees every day of your life. You're free to do that! But if I were you, Timothy—" her chin trembled again "—I would judge a little less and pray a little more in thanksgiving that there are those of us out there willing to do what has to be done to protect all that for you."

"We do not judge. That is the Lord's to do."

"But you reject—"

"Silence! *Behaf di!* We are not ungrateful for our lives, here, Annie," he scolded, "but we are still targets of small minds and empty hearts and as long as you are here, taking refuge from the kind of men who would do this to your husband, we are in danger."

TIMOTHY LEFT THEN. Ann followed him to the door as he reiterated his conditions. She stood there long after he had gone, looking out the window, seeing nothing.

"Ann?"

Her head dipped low. She dragged the polka-dot kerchief off her head, unpinned her braids and forced her chin up as she turned to answer him.

Despite the care she had given him round the clock for these days and nights, she could not get used to him lying there half-naked, his powerful, bruised chest with all that lush brown hair bared to her.

You would think she had never left this place. You would think she had never seen a naked man. You would think she was some other woman than the one who had seduced him with callous, calculated intent in Manny's garage. You would think she was still twelve and not thirty-two.

Her body knew better. Her hands knew. Her heart knew.

She took her foolish self in hand and met his eyes. "You should get some rest now."

"Why do you do that?"

"Why do I do what?"

"Pin up your hair."

"It's what's done here. I agreed to abide by the rules."

"And then you lied? About us. Ann?"

She could only do this if she laughed. "I promised to abide by the rules after I had already lied."

"Did you really tell your brother we were married?"

"I told him you were my husband."

"You should have told me." He cracked a grin that gave *iniquity* new meaning, but it faded soon enough. "We've lost so much time already."

She sat down again in the plain, hard chair beside the bed. The gas heater was turned low, and there was so little space between them that she could feel his body heat. In the silence it was his male scent, his body washed with homemade soap that stole away her wits.

She had not lost so much time. She had taken her small liberties.

Feasted on his lean, muscled, utterly masculine body with her eyes.

Shaped her hand to his chest, telling herself it was only his heartbeat she needed to gauge, the depth of the bruise that spanned the width of her hand.

Run her fingertips over the bony prominence of his pelvis…

And there was always a small warning voice asking, *What carnal sin is this, Annie Tschetter? What dangerous game are you playing? What if, when he wakes, he remembers?* More often, *This can never be.* She had not experienced that voice in many years.

"Are you going to tell me why?" he asked, rousing her from the voice inside her.

She swallowed. "We should talk about what happened that night, J.D. Who came gunning for you—"

He looked at her. Pain creased his forehead, made gravel of his voice. "Tell me, Ann."

"It's nothing."

His eyes burned into hers. *Are you lying now, Annie Tschetter?*

"Timothy had already refused me twice. He told me to take you to a hospital. When I told him I couldn't do that…well." Her shrug was more shiver. "It doesn't matter. I was tired and desperate. He couldn't believe I would persist, so he asked me who you are to me. It just came out. My instinct must have been that if you were someone who mattered very much to me, it might make a difference. Might make him change his mind. So that's what I told him."

His left eye pinched shut in a pain as he hiked himself up again in the feather bed. "Guess it worked, huh?"

"Thorne—"

"Why did you leave?"

"It's very…complicated." Her feelings had always come at each other like predators fighting to the death over the scrap of her being. She wanted desperately to be loved, but she wasn't, not for herself, not for the things that set her apart, which were anathema to colony life. She wanted just as desperately to be set free, but the notion was at first so foreign, and later so terrifying that she would abandon herself and try again to make them love her, whatever it took.

She could never pull it off.

"Ann?" His beautiful brown eyes, glazed with pain, bore into her. "Tell me."

His intensity alarmed her. In this place, there was no tolerance for such intimate, self-indulgent thought, let alone conversation, but J.D. would not rest until he knew. He would not leave her be, let it go, this thing between them. He would not believe her when she said she would finally disappoint him. And she could not go on stealing her sweet, sensual liberties and not end up tearing her soul in two. She had to make him understand.

"I don't know how to tell you what it's like here." She had never tried to explain it, never once in all her years on the outside spoken of her old life. "The women here would tell you that they have it far better than on the outside. They share all their work. They never have to worry who will look after the children. When they marry, they don't have to consider if he'll be a good provider because the colony provides for every need. There is always food on the table here. Where they will live, what they will wear, what work they will do, everything is settled for them.

"There is no such thing as privacy or individual possessions here—nothing that won't fit into a chest. No one owns a car, no one dresses to suit themselves,

no one grows up and leaves to become a fireman or
an astronaut or a doctor or lawyer. No one would ask
a child what he wanted to be when he grows up. He
wouldn't even understand the question. What he
wants is to grow old enough to drive the tractor. And
what girls learn is that they are inferior in every way,
that they must obey the boys. And if there are too
many Annas or Marys, we go first by our father's
names. Jakob Anna, Joseph Anna, Peter Anna.''

Once started, she hardly knew how to stop, maybe
because it was so hard to arrive at what mattered
most to her.

She shrugged. He readjusted the pillow behind his
head, but she knew his attention never wavered despite his pain.

''There's so much more, but the point is that I
never fit in here. I couldn't. It's as if God was making
a joke when he gave me to them. I can't fault them.
They are as happy in their faith and their community
as they expect to be on earth. If you asked any one
of them how many close friends they have, they
would tell you hundreds. That's how it is for them.
They have each other to depend upon in all things.
They have no doubts, no questions. They know their
reward is laid up in heaven. They believe that there
is no hope of that for me, but it is what they always
wanted for me.''

Her hands, so flighty, fell to her lap. She felt the
sting of tears, couldn't believe after all this time she
could still feel so vulnerable. ''I—''

''Ann…what gives?'' He struggled up a bit, the
effort betraying itself in the lines around his eyes.
''It isn't like you to beat around the bush like this.
Spit it out.''

"All right." She sat straighter, made herself look into his eyes and condense the flurry of her thoughts to the point that needed to be made. "They wanted to save me from myself, too."

He stared at her, his intensity sharpened. "I musta missed something. See, back there in that chop shop I thought it was you saving me from myself."

He tried to sit up, but then exhaled sharply. His eyes rolled back and then his lids fluttered shut. She could hear his teeth grinding. "I think—" He tried to pull at the bandage near his armpit. His words slurred. "I think I musta started something bleeding again."

She tipped over her chair getting to the bed, then crawled up over the comforter beside him to see what he had done. She saw the stain of fresh blood without even having to remove the bandage.

"You are bleeding. Hold on. Lie still, I'll be right back." She had piles of fresh gauze and disinfectant no farther away than the sideboard behind her wooden chair. She grabbed the supplies, laid them at his side, then crawled back across the bed shoved tight against the wall.

Removing the bandage, she had to restrain him from trying to help her. It was that kind of movement that had probably started the bleeding in the first place. She cut through the gauze rather than trying to get it over his head, then found the place beneath his arm nearest the thatch of hair where a single stitch drawn too tight had broken.

She held a thick wad of gauze to the bleeding with her left hand, her hip lodged next to his, her legs curled to her side, balancing herself with her right hand on the other side of his body. His eyes closed tight, his jaw clenched shut against the pain.

She kept tight the compress for a couple of more minutes, then let go to cut a new length of fabric for bandaging. When she had it arranged slinglike to keep pressure, he could lower his arm, and the tightness in his face eased.

With his wounds, she could always do what had to be done. But she could never finish without tears coming to her eyes for his pain, or for how close he had come to dying.

See, I thought it was you saving me…

She leaned a bit to her left, counterbalancing, letting her right hand go to his forehead where she stroked his hair back from his face, again and again and again, crooning comforting nonsense.

"Ann." *Like a prayer.* He lifted his right hand, perhaps to touch her outstretched arm. She would never know, for his fingers brushed her breast and she forgot to breathe. The pain eased from his brow, his lips fell open. A tiny vein on his forehead pulsed. She had only to lower her arm, to leave off stroking his brow to end his accidental touch, but the want of it rose up like a craziness in her blood.

She couldn't seem to help herself. Her memories of his kiss those long months ago after Christo McCourt met his father made her weak with longing. Memories she had been able to shut out in Seattle, but not here, not living with him as she was, as if he were her husband and she his bride, twenty-four hours a day. Not here.

Here in this room, in this colony where she had grown up, she wasn't so much the streetwise, blush-proof, seen-it-all Detective Ann Calder, but Annie

Tschetter, the girl who could not be molded and shaped to suit her elders, who could not be made to stop her imaginings or sacrifice her sense of a self, a girl who wanted to want something for herself alone.

This she wanted. The sensations of J.D.'s hand on her breast, stroking her, cupping her, lifting the weight of her into his hand through layers of fabric, all so slowly with such care and erotic sensibility that she could have died.

To endure it she fixed her eyes at a point on the stark white wall over his head. Her hand cradled his cheek. So long as she kept her arm outstretched, the keen pleasure need never end. *Let this moment never end...*

"Look at me, Annie. Look at me."

She dragged her gaze to her hand, to his lips, his eyes. His thumbnail grazed fabric. Her breasts tingled, her nipples rose exquisitely, visibly tight. She swore, watching herself in the reflection of his eyes, that she could feel the pluck of each tiny thread by his thumbnail, and anticipate the next, till her nipple was mounted and pleasure too intense to bear broke through her, drizzling, dark, deep.

"Give us a chance, Annie Tschetter," he uttered. "Give us a chance." He took her hand from his face and took it low on his body to the one sweet liberty she hadn't already stolen, and groaned. He shifted his body and lifted his hand to her nape and dragged her down into kisses more tender and heated and wet with desire than she had ever known.

Give us a chance, Annie Tschetter.

Chapter Six

The cold hit him like a wall.

The only time J.D. had been out of the book-binder's hut in six days was for trips to the outhouse, but he'd watched the comings and goings out his window, so he pulled up his collar, took his best guess and headed for the central colony building. His sling abandoned, his body only beginning to heal, he needed real food, and he needed it now.

Ann was nowhere to be found.

Frustration shadowed him like carrion birds hovering over an animal carcass. He thought he understood Ann. He could see why she'd left this place. If the clash with her brother hadn't brought it all into focus, her meandering explanation of her life in the colony had pretty much made it come clear.

As clear to him as her bottom line. She wouldn't be saved from herself. Not by them, not my him.

She would not be discounted or have her native intelligence stifled or barter her right to think for herself for anything. Not for her place in the Lord's Ark here on earth or the certainty of a blissful hereafter.

He just hadn't quite gotten it through his admittedly thick skull that to give in to her feelings for him made her crazy. To wade into the morass of desire between them, to go with what she wanted— no, he thought—to *take* what she wanted, was to her the same thing as "submitting to a man," as Timothy had so quaintly put it.

Her freedom was not negotiable. What she felt for him, what went on between them, didn't stand a chance. Such things were fleeting, as insubstantial to her as the frost on the glass by his bed in the book- binder's hut.

Eventually, she believed, he would make demands on her she couldn't live with, and she would disap- point him in her failure to conform.

He needed time away from her anyway, time to think, time to consider what he was going to do, because his problems went way beyond Ann and the bookbinder's hut, where bibles and hymnals and German-language schoolbooks languished for repair.

He still could not remember anything that had hap- pened before the shooting.

That was all Ann was willing to talk about.

Who had he seen in the hours leading up to the attempt on his life? What had he done? Where had he gone? Why that particular night and not all the nights that had gone before?

Ann had questioned him, goaded him, played as- sociation games, any trick, over and over again to stimulate his memory of the hours leading up to the shooting.

Nothing.

He knew he had alienated people he'd once re- spected. He'd violated the code that no one ever talked about but everyone knew. A cop never ratted out another cop.

Never. There could be no excuse. If a cop got caught on the take or somehow burned himself being stupid or outright blatant, then he deserved what he got. J.D. believed the dirty cops he'd exposed for TruthSayers acting on their own agendas *had* burned themselves. They could not have been relieved of duty without cause, and that bar was set high. He'd met the level of proof, but he was in a small minority of cops who believed that.

But he'd been at it for months, and the ones under scrutiny knew who they were. If any one of them was going to take him out, they'd have done it before they wound up off the force and out of a pension.

He didn't believe in coincidence, which led him and Ann to conclude that sometime in the hours before the shooting, he had rung some bell that someone with considerable clout wanted unrung.

So yesterday came the decision. They'd both known it was time to act, time to find out by whatever other means than J.D.'s memory they could find. Ann had gone to her brother Timothy's office and returned with a cell phone—another modern tool meant for the purposes of running the colony business. She'd handed it to him, gone over again what they had concluded.

''Are you convinced it would be a mistake to call Matt or Garrett?''

''Not a doubt in my mind. Whoever is gunning for me will be watching both of them.'' The same logic went for her friends, people she trusted. To let anyone know where they were would be a dangerous burden.

''Rand is still the best possibility, then?'' she'd asked.

She already knew, because they'd been through these alternatives before, that J.D. had grown up with Martin Rand, and that as a federal court judge, Rand was in a fairly powerful position to help. And aside from Matt and Garrett, no one knew of J.D.'s friendship with a federal magistrate.

But Rand's powerful position was also the problem. Professionally, Rand had to stand back, at an arm's length from any involvement in goings-on that had the potential of winding up in the judicial system.

J.D. grimaced, even now, a day later, at his lapses. He hadn't even known what day it was. Ann told him Wednesday, he'd said Rand would be in court. She'd had to remind him he'd told her Rand was on sabbatical.

She urged him to try Rand at home. "We really do need to know what's going on, whether they've caught the shooter or have a line on it. Rand is surely following the case. He has to be worried about you. And if he even suspects the press aren't being given all the details, he can easily find out what the status is."

"No matter what he says, Ann, we've got to come up with a plan to get out of here."

He sat bare-chested with his back to the wall on the feather bed and dialed his best friend.

He picked up on the third ring. "Martin Rand."

"Marty, J.D."

After a moment of shocked hesitation, Rand asked, "Where are you?"

"Safe for the moment."

"Good God, man, are you okay? There was one hell of a lot of blood—"

He reassured Rand that he was on the mend. "What I need to know, Marty, is whether the cops have arrested the shooters." Describing the total blackout in his memory of the hours preceding the assault, he gave Rand an idea of his problem. "Thing is, I must have rung someone's chimes, but I don't have a clue."

Rand cleared his throat. "You were here for a while that afternoon. We had a couple of beers. Do you remember being here?"

"No. What did we talk about?"

"The futility of Vorees's trial, mostly." Rand went on. "J.D., look. We all knew you might as well have had a target tattooed on your back. You've got to go into protective custody. Tell me where you are. I can arrange—"

"Marty? No. Not only no, *hell no.*"

"J.D., man! Come on. You're not thinking clearly. You have to be smart about this. The marshal service certainly isn't out to get you."

"You didn't say whether the cops have made an arrest or not."

"They haven't. I don't know if they have any leads, but what does it matter? As long as you're out there, you're a sitting duck."

Better a sitting duck, J.D. thought, on his own terms than in a shooting gallery provided compliments of the U.S. marshals. "All I need is the inside information, Marty. If I knew who did this, I might have a chance of figuring out why. Can you get it for me or not?"

"Of course. It may take a day of two. Will I be able to reach you at this phone?"

A nasty shiver had gone through J.D.'s body. He'd

reached out and taken Ann's hand for a little human warmth. Of course Marty would have caller ID on his phone. But the thought of anyone knowing his whereabouts, even his oldest friend, made J.D.'s stomach knot.

He could count on one hand the number of people who knew he and Rand were friends, or that it was Martin Rand who had gone to the trouble of getting J.D. the interview that led to his position on the U.S. attorney's TruthSayers task force undercover team.

Ames and Everly went all the way back to Telluride with J.D. and Rand, so they knew, as did Garrett and Matt. But as in the old saying, three can keep a secret if two are dead, J.D. had developed a healthy respect for the way the TruthSayers seemed inevitably to uncover obscure ties, arcane information, the telling details that enabled their agenda.

But then he thought, how paranoid was he going to allow himself to become? He'd told Rand instead, "I'll have to get back to you. I don't know where I'll be twenty-four hours from now."

And then he'd hung up. But he didn't like what his gut was telling him at all.

Still didn't. He was either paranoid, or Rand— J.D. stopped dead in his tracks in the wind-hardened snow with dead-on certainty that the same flagrantly mistrustful thought had occurred to him before.

But when? As he sat there at Marty's place drinking beers and shooting holes in the prosecutor's already plague-ridden case against Vorees?

The bitter cold made his head pound worse than ever. If he was growing paranoid, he had reason. The gunshot wound at his armpit burned with every move and he still couldn't really breathe right. He knew it was healing, but he couldn't remember a time when his threshold for pain had been so pathetic, or his brain so addled, or his instincts firing off such unworthy, impenetrable warnings.

God, but he was hungry. As soon as he had something substantial in his gut, he might be able to think more clearly.

His breath made small puffs of steam in the frigid cold. He reached the door of the central building, took a deep breath and expelled one last cloud. He had no idea what to expect, and even in so benign a place as this farm, he felt his guard lever up.

The door opened directly into a kitchen that reminded him of school cafeterias. Several girls, young women, maybe fifteen to twenty years old, apparently finishing up the mealtime dishes, stood chattering and joking among themselves. One of them turned toward him with a towel and a handful of industrial-size cooking utensils in her hands.

At the sight of him, her ladles and spatulas clattered to the floor, and in the unnerving silence they stood still as statues, regarding him with a mixture of wide-eyed curiosity and dread.

He'd scared the living daylights out of them. "I'm sorry. I didn't mean to startle you." He moved toward the one bending in her deep flush and confusion to retrieve the utensils. "Let me help—"

"No!" She clasped her hands as if to pray for some divine intervention. "No...please. I can do it." She crouched low and began snatching up the offending utensils, but her eyes kept darting in his direction and among the others. It was as if the devil himself had sauntered into their kitchen.

He knelt and picked up a cooking fork that had

skittered beyond reach across the pale yellow linoleum. The girl took it from him with a nervous smile.

He thought if he returned her smile, she might faint dead away, so he only asked, "Would it be all right if I made myself a sandwich?"

"Oh no," she uttered, more upset than before. "I...menfolk don't..."

"Please." One of the older girls stepped bravely forward. He thought his whiskered chin was about as close to his eyes as she could manage looking. "I will make you a sandwich if you will wait please in...over there." She pointed through another door to cafeteria-style tables set in perfect rows.

J.D. nodded. "Of course. I'm sorry. I didn't mean—"

"It is no trouble." She pointed again. "Over there. The far tables, not the near."

He nodded again through the thunderbolts in his head, feeling absurdly out of place. He went where he had been directed and sat uneasily on a bench, which he understood must be the men's side of the dining room. He heard the urgent whispering of the flock of girls from the kitchen and knew he'd violated territory. The brave one, her eyes never meeting his, brought him two ham sandwiches, the bread slathered thickly with butter, and a large helping of chunky applesauce.

"Will this do?"

"It's fine. Thank you very much." He had to get out of here. "I don't want to disturb you. Is there somewhere warm I can go—"

"The horse barn." Ann's brother Timothy stood in the doorway, his expression as nearly murderous as J.D. imagined he was capable. "Out the door you came in. A hundred paces to the south."

He stood, plate of sandwiches and applesauce and spoon in hand, and went out the way he had come, having to pass by Timothy to do it.

He trekked across the compound to the barn, noticing all kinds of unexpectedly modern fixtures for the first time. He lifted the bar on the barn door and let himself inside. The smell of it, hay and horseflesh and leather, brought him foursquare with the scents and memories, not all good, of his childhood. He felt himself go light-headed. Leaning against the inside of the barn door, he stood there waiting for the dizziness to pass.

Praying the dizziness would pass.

It took a while.

He sat on a bale of hay by the horse stalls and consumed the sandwiches by the meager light of the windows, substituting his fingers for a spoon for the applesauce. He could have eaten two or three more sandwiches but he wasn't going back to that kitchen for seconds.

He leaned back against a post for a few moments, taking in the quiet, the gentle sough of horses breathing, while he let the food settle enough to imagine he felt sated.

His thoughts went back soon enough to the dilemma he now faced. Once in a while he felt a wisp of frozen air coming through the windows, keeping the gas-heated barn from growing too hot. His eyes had become more accustomed to the meager light filtering through, so when he spotted a stack of horse blankets on a shelf near the ledge, he took one and spread it out on the bale, then eased his handgun from the waistband of his jeans.

Sitting crosswise on the bale of hay, he began methodically to break down the weapon. While it could be done and back together inside sixty seconds, he took his time.

The ritual had the effect of focusing his thoughts, but failed to deliver up what he needed most to remember. But whether he could remember or not, he would have to act, and soon. He couldn't stay here much longer. On his feet again, however unsteady and ill prepared to deal with the outside, he expected the colony elders to turn them out soon. Timothy was right. As long as J.D. and Ann remained here, the colony itself was in danger.

BY THE SECOND TIME Martin Rand called Matt Guiliani, Ann Calder's car had been found abandoned along state highway 101 south of Tillamook, Oregon. Blood in the back seat matched Thorne's known ABO and Rh types, and while Calder's prints had been identified, the latents off the steering wheel had ID'd a felon with a rap sheet two pages long as well.

Among the various law enforcement agencies involved, it was believed Calder and Thorne had not gone south at all. Either the felon had stolen her car, which, given its vintage, made no sense, or else he'd been paid handsomely to take the car and drive as far as he could get in the direction opposite the way J.D. and Ann had headed. Her car was nothing but a decoy.

Matt had decided there really was no need to worry about Ann and J.D., right up until Rand called again. Something about the conversation bothered the hell out of him. He'd been at home, making himself a panful of lasagna, but got the call on his pager. The number wasn't one he recognized, nor the one from which Rand had called before.

"Guiliani."

"Matt, this is Rand."

He'd waited, trying to identify the background noise, deciding the clink of glass and level of voices put Rand in a bar or restaurant.

"J.D. called me this afternoon."

"He's okay, then?" Matt asked.

"He's alive, anyway."

"Where?"

"Some farm outside Cold Springs, Montana."

"He told you?" That was it, Matt thought, looking back on the brief exchange. The moment he'd begun to get truly bad vibes, because Rand said yes, J.D. had disclosed his location. Matt didn't believe it. He'd worked so closely with J. D. Thorne over some forty-seven months that he knew better. Knew Thorne's instincts as well as he knew his own.

There was no way that in his situation J.D. would have given up his whereabouts even to his mother.

Rand wanted to go through with his plan to send in federal marshals. J.D. had apparently refused. Rand hoped Matt would entertain the possibility of going along, in that way reassuring J.D. that he would be safe and not giving himself up to Truth-Sayers in the guise of legitimate law enforcement officers.

Rand was in effect asking Matt to vouch for men he didn't know. It wasn't going to happen. Someone wanted J. D. Thorne dead, probably Ann as well at this point, and until Matt knew that threat had been taken out, there was no way he'd intervene even, maybe especially, on Martin Rand's say-so.

But Matt would have to do something, and soon. By the time J.D. learned that Rand had not kept his trap shut, however well intended, whatever his motives, it might be too late.

SITTING THERE in the half-lit barn considering his narrow spectrum of options, J.D. picked up the barrel of his gun and ran his thumb along its length as if he had a chamois. Then, what he least needed to happen, happened. A handful of teenage boys sneaked into the barn through a door that in his stupor J.D. hadn't even spotted.

The boys crowded around before it occurred to his clouded mind that he should at least have flipped the edges of the horse blanket over the pieces of his gun. Just as alike in their black jeans and white shirts and dark-colored coats as the girls were in their dresses, they stood staring at, or admiring, the pieces of the gun.

One of them sank to his haunches. He looked a lot like Ann's brother Timothy, but he could as easily belong to one of her other brothers or sisters.

"That a real gun?"

"Real as they come."

"Is it broken? 'Cuz I can usually figure out how things go together."

J.D. shook his head. "It's not broken. I'm sure you could put it back together, but I don't think it would be a good idea. In fact, it's probably not a good idea for you guys to be here at all."

"Yeah. We'll be in for a strapping." The six of

them nodded solemnly, but none made a move to leave. "We're cool with that."

"You are, huh?" He couldn't begin to count the times he'd done what he damn well pleased, knowing good and well that his uncle Jess would tan his ever-lovin' hide.

They all sat down cross-legged and introduced themselves. All but one were Tschetters. The one called Paul piped up. "Me and Josh saw that *Lethal Weapon* movie playing on a television in the Kmart. Nobody knows," he confided, "'cept now you. You're a cop too, huh?"

"Yeah. But it's not like in the movies."

"You musta done some way-cool things," Michael, the smallest boy said, his tone filled with reverence. "You got a gun."

As if owning a gun imparted cool. These kids weren't nearly so untouched as J.D. imagined their elders believed, though every bit as mistakenly taken as typical kids with the romance of guns. He wanted to answer responsibly, take some of the edge off their awe. He had few doubts that Timothy would show up here any second as he had in the kitchen, and J.D.'s head was reeling without even thinking what that would mean. To Ann. To himself.

"A gun is not a cool thing." But his hands moved with such familiarity and speed reassembling his piece that "cool" was in the eyes of these beholders, nothing they were going to take on his say-so.

He shoved the gun into the pocket of his sheepskin coat, the least cool thing he could do with it. Taking a different, tamer tack, he told them a Wild West cop story even Guiliani thought was pretty cool.

"Trapped some bank robbers once. It was pretty cool how we ambushed them in the mountains."

He could tell from the disappointment in their eager eyes that this was poor fodder compared to Gibson and Glover blowing up buildings and enduring spectacular car crashes. "That's about as exciting as it gets in real life."

"How much money was there?" the little one, Michael, asked.

"A half million and change."

Paul whistled through a gap in his front teeth. "That's enough to buy out our whole farm."

"Pretty close," J.D. answered, though he thought half a million would only buy the farm machinery. Whatever else Ann's people rejected of the outside, they purchased and used modern equipment.

"So, how'd you do it?" Josh asked.

"Old Indian trick. Mirrors."

Paul scoffed. "Indians didn't have mirrors."

"No, but they had mica, silver, shiny things like that."

"What'd they do? Wink the sun at each other?"

"Exactly. They'd use whatever they had to reflect the sun so they could signal to each other over great distances." He took a few straws of hay and illustrated a trap for unwary settlers moving wagon trains through mountain passes. "You can pull off an ambush a couple of ways, but either way, you have to seal off any chance of escape. In this case, if one side swoops in before the other side is ready or in place, then they leave open an avenue of escape."

"'n is that how you caught the bank robbers?" one of the boys asked, wide-eyed.

"That's exactly how we caught them. Plus, we had

horses, and they didn't. They were planning to hike out and disappear with the—''

He cut himself short when he heard the bar go up on the barn door and saw against the light the dark towering figure of a man, and a woman, Ann, J.D. thought, at his side. The harsh winter sun glaring off acres of snow sent a stabbing pain through his head, but what struck J.D. hard was the boys shrinking one by one to the ground, unnaturally silent, their faces transformed into masks of resignation and doom.

He sensed trouble, could nearly smell Ann's distress, but nothing bad or evil had happened here and all he could think was that he had never seen anything like this. What kind of kids were these that they didn't get up and make a run for it?

''You see now?'' came a mean and spiteful voice. ''Is this how you repay us?'' He grabbed Ann by her upper arm and half shoved, half dragged her with him out of the glare of the sunlight and into the deep shadows of the barn. As if drawn by a magnet, the shadows filled with colony men in near silence behind the furious bare-faced man dragging Ann along with him. ''This is the kind of man you bring into our midst, sitting here in the dark like the devil, spinning stories of the outside to seduce our children, make the devil's work glamorous and exciting in their untutored eyes?''

''Samuel—''

''Is this what you want, Peter Annie?'' He all but shook her. ''To destroy us all? Is that what you want?''

''Samuel, stop it,'' she hissed, trying in vain to shake his manic grip on her arm. ''He means no harm, nothing like that—''

"Excuse me." J.D. rose, and though he interrupted with such polite finesse, no one mistook his anger. "Samuel, is it? Kindly take your hand off my wife."

He defied J.D. with a snarling expression, but Samuel let his hand fall away.

"What's going on here?" Timothy demanded, stepping forward. "Samuel?"

"The boys failed to return to English school after their *recess*." He uttered the word with outright contempt for the English teacher who fostered such lax and ill-conceived use of school time. "I found them here, with him, showing off his gun, filling their minds with—"

Ann interrupted his venomous diatribe. "Timothy, this is my fault. He doesn't know our...your customs. I didn't tell him your—"

"Ann, that's ludicrous!" J.D. cut her off. He didn't know why she would stand there assuming the blame any more than he understood why she had allowed Samuel to manhandle her. "You had nothing to do with this."

She gave him a fierce look. "You don't understand."

"I understand what is my responsibility."

"No, you don't. This is not your concern. This has nothing to do with you."

"What should we expect?" Samuel spat the words. "He doesn't even have the control of his wife."

"Silence!" Timothy commanded. "I sent him here to eat in peace and quiet. And you are no one to judge the intentions of another."

Samuel flushed darkly. His Adam's apple pitched

wildly as he pointed again at Ann. "She is the cause."

"You are the cause of your own trouble, Samuel," Timothy decreed. "You will not let go. She is a woman. You should know better than to continue in this self-indulgent behavior. You make a spectacle of yourself. You are the one who, day after day, year in and year out, continues to make yourself into a martyr. Now go!"

Trembling with rage, Samuel turned and stalked through the small crowd of assembled men in their black hats and severe expressions.

In the instant when the men parted, a much older man, his face thinned with age, his white beard betraying the tremoring of his chin, his eyes fixed on Ann, caught her attention. J.D. watched her posture tighten and her face go pale as a ghost, and he knew this must be her father, silently confronting his wanton, runaway daughter for the first time in too many years.

The silent showdown went on interminably, Timothy witness to it, letting it grow, letting his father see what greater damage Ann had brought down upon them.

J.D. knew he was witnessing the genesis of that hard-as-flint, unforgiving part of Ann that had attracted him so powerfully from the start, that set her apart from every other woman he had ever known. The part that suggested she knew some things were unforgivable, that would not fail to call a spade a spade.

He could not believe in a God that would have this man turn such loathing on his daughter.

This was unforgivable.

He watched her standing up to the scathing, silent judgment, till he couldn't take it anymore.

"Mr. Tschetter. Sir." The old man dragged his condemning gaze off Ann, substituting J.D. "No man looks on my wife in that way."

Chapter Seven

He knew he was exploiting Ann's lie in ways she had never intended. He knew it would make her mad to come roaring in to her defense. He didn't care. He wouldn't tolerate anyone treating her like this. "Maybe you would like to take up your anger with me. As for the boys—"

"Thorne, don't," she began to object, as he'd known she would, but her eldest brother interrupted.

"You." Timothy turned to Ann. "You have nothing to say that we want to hear. Nor do you," he said to J.D. "It is not your place to answer for her. Or for the disobedience of our sons."

Exchanging glances with Ann, with nothing else to do, J.D. let the disaster play out. The thing with Samuel alarmed him. He suspected it had to do with Ann, with ancient history. But Ann was right. He didn't understand any of it.

Timothy spoke to the boys, not in anger, but in resignation, as if this infraction had been a temptation he might have expected to be too powerful to resist. "Go back to school. Afterward, you will be dealt with."

The boys got up as one and filed out of the door

through which Samuel had hauled Ann, and as if by some unheard command, the other men trailed out as well. All except Timothy and the preacher Wilmes, who stood a few moments, his head lowered in thought or prayer.

Wilmes could contain himself no longer. "You see, now, Peter Annie, what trouble rains down on us when we allow the outside in? You must leave us, and you must do it today."

Ann started to protest, but Timothy drew himself up and warned her with a look to say nothing. "No," he said. "We do not want your blood on our hands. There will be no ultimatums. But you must look into your heart, Annie Tschetter, and know what harm your presence brings even though that is not your intention. Use the telephone in my office. Make other arrangements. Surely in your world there must be a few honorable men who can help you out of the troubles you are in."

One of the younger men, closely resembling Timothy, let himself back into the barn. "Timothy..." The preacher and Ann's brother turned toward him. "It's Samuel. He's taken off down the road. Do you want me to go after him?"

Ann regarded her brother closely, but again, Timothy's head bowed low. "No. I am tired of dealing with him. Samuel will do what Samuel does, and he will soon know the consequences."

Timothy gave one last imploring look to Ann, then turned and walked out of the barn, his arm around the shoulders of the preacher to whom he would have to answer himself.

ONLY THE YOUNGER MEN lingered. One was her brother, a younger, slighter version of Timothy. No gray had yet crept into his beard, nor any sternness about his eyes. Ann spoke softly to him. "Andreas, you should go, too."

"Annie...I know. I'm sorry about Pop. And Samuel. If there's anything I can do to help the two of you—" He broke off, looking at J.D., then came forward and offered his hand. "I'm Andreas Tschetter, one of Ann's brothers."

He shook hands. "J. D. Thorne. Ann's—"

"Husband. I know."

J.D. stuck his fingers in the pocket of his jeans. "That was your father, then?"

Andreas nodded, but spoke mostly to Ann. "Samuel rubs Pop's nose in it every day with his bare face."

"Rubs his nose in what?"

A look passed between her and Andreas. She felt acutely aware of J.D.'s attention. "I haven't told J.D. about...about Samuel."

"Maybe you should."

"I will. But you should go now, before there's more trouble, okay?"

"You come to me if you need anything. I won't do anything to defy Micah or Timothy, but if I can help you get out of here, you come to me. I have friends south from here from my tourism."

J.D. frowned. "What's that?"

Andreas grinned. "It's what we call it when we leave the colony for a while. Most of us do it for a year or so at least."

"Most boys," Ann corrected softly.

Andreas agreed, a little sheepish. "We raise a little hell, get a bellyful of what it's like to live on the outside. Sometimes we make friends worth keeping in touch with. These I'm talking about are good people, nothing to do with TruthSayers, and I know they would help you.''

Andreas gave Ann a stiff, awkward, emotional hug, then turned to go, but as he reached the door to the barn, an uneasy thought came to her.

''Andreas?''

He turned back.

''Where will Samuel go?''

Her brother shrugged. ''Probably catch a ride into town. Why?''

''What does he do there? Why did Timothy say he was tired of dealing with Samuel?''

''He drinks himself into a stupor—'' Andreas's handsome face grew fearful as it occurred to him that Samuel could be a threat to them all. He walked back to her. ''Oh, Ann. I'm sorry. He might be a problem.''

Ann swallowed. ''Surely he doesn't talk about colony business.''

''A man is never in control of himself when he drinks like that, Ann,'' Andreas answered worriedly, as if he couldn't imagine she might know how a man got with enough liquor inside him. ''Samuel has gotten drunk on his butt a couple of times over the years.'' Worry crossed his bearded face like the shadows of clouds on the earth. ''If he shoots off his mouth about your being here, the Lord only knows where it will lead. Even after you're gone, there could be repercussions.''

J.D. sat back down on the bale. ''The chances are pretty remote, Andreas, that there will be anyone sitting in a bar with Samuel who would even recognize our names.''

Andreas nodded, though clearly, he still didn't like it. ''I'll talk to Timothy.'' He saw her begin to shake her head. ''Don't worry. Timothy won't argue the point. I will go after him. I promise you, Ann.'' He took her chin between his fingers. ''I'll go after him.''

''Thank you.'' She gave him a kiss on the cheek, for which he looked to her so tenderly, with such longing and pain in his eyes for her absence all these years that tears sprang to her own. ''Go on. And thank you again.''

''It's nothing.''

After he had gone, J.D. lowered his head into both his hands. After a few seconds, he looked up at her.

''Were you close to Andreas?''

She nodded. ''We were closest in age. He was five when I was born. He always looked out for me. Timothy was more a father to me than our father was.''

''What about your mother? Your sisters?''

''My mother died when I was born. As for sisters...'' A lump filled her throat. She'd had seven of them as well, but now she couldn't even remember what they had looked like. ''They're all gone from here. When a woman marries, she moves away to her husband's colony.'' She shook off the useless emotion, making that her mission. She didn't like the worry creasing his forehead. ''Andreas will do what he said, Thorne.''

He nodded. ''Probably not any big deal.''

''Do you really believe that?''

He shrugged. ''No one knows where we are. It would have to be a pretty wild coincidence.'' He thought about Rand knowing by his caller ID, and told her what he'd been thinking on his way to the colony kitchens.

"So that's how all this came about?"

"I'm sorry, Ann. I woke up so hungry my gut was growling. You were gone, I didn't know where. If I'd known what kind of brouhaha I was about to get into—"

"Don't apologize, J.D. Really. If it wasn't one thing, it would be another." She gave a bittersweet smile. "The boys would have found a way to talk to you even if they'd had to wait outside the outhouse door."

She came near and knelt on the floor by the bale, at his knees. "You've gone white as a sheet. Are you okay?"

"Dizzy. Mostly I can ignore the pain under my arm, but my head won't quit spinning." Elbows on his knees, he rested his head in his hands. She put her arms around him, let his head rest on her shoulder, let her lips come down on his hair.

He wanted this nightmare to end. She wanted only to change the venue. With each passing day, tending to his needs, his food, scrubbing the blood from his sheepskin vest, washing and folding and mending his clothes…playing house with J. D. Thorne, trading long and sultry looks for kisses and intimacies, her hand here, his lips there, she began to imagine such a lifetime.

But this was no paradise, nor in their lives away from here would they ever have such time together again. She knew it was pure fantasy, stolen moments in the wake of an attempt on his life.

His frustration only grew worse with every passing

hour. He tried to hide it from her but she knew what he was made of, how much he wanted to regain those blacked-out hours, how badly he needed to know what had set off his attackers. If he knew that, he stood a decent chance of outliving the threat. And if he didn't, well, failure wasn't an option, wasn't even to be found in J. D. Thorne's vocabulary.

The knot on the back of his head had shrunk to the size of a small child's fist. It could be days before his memory returned and his head stopped throbbing. If the memory came back at all.

She thought he was lucky to be alive at all.

She put her hands on his shoulders and sat on her legs, her skirt forming a circle about her on the floor. She looked up at him. The few moments in her arms seemed to have eased his pain, lessened the degree of paleness in his face. "J.D., do you want to talk to Andreas about his friends? Call Rand back? Try Matt or Garrett?"

He shook his head. She suspected this was the reason he'd come out to the barn, to make some kind of decision, but he asked first about Samuel. "Tell me what just happened here."

She looked down, staring at her hands in her lap a moment. "Samuel Pullman is a powder keg, in the way of a stray spark."

He sighed heavily.

Guilt came down hard on her. Was there no place safe on earth for them? But she couldn't succumb to unavailing sentiment. "When I interrupted you and I said you didn't understand, what I meant was that I didn't want either one of us to say anything that would antagonize Samuel any more than he already was."

"Is it you, Ann? Is he nursing some old grudge?"

She nodded. Her eyes lowered, then returned, resigned, to his. "My father had arranged that Samuel would marry me. When I refused, he…" She shrugged. "He wasn't happy. He felt that he'd been humiliated in front of the entire colony—and he was, even though I tried to say it wasn't him, that I would never marry at all.

"It's the worst kind of sin around here," she went on when she knew J.D. wasn't going to comment, "not to forgive one who has sinned against you, as he believed I had. It's even cause for banning to be so stubborn and hold on to your grievances, but he has apparently never gotten over it. That's why he shaves. Married men wear a beard, or men who by Samuel's age haven't married for whatever reason."

"That's what Andreas meant when he said that Samuel rubs your father's nose in it every day?"

"Yes. Samuel's bare face is a constant admonition."

"So when you told them I was your husband…?"

She nodded. "I was completely without a thought. When I decided to come here, it never occurred to me that Samuel would not have married someone else. He never entered my mind. Then, when I got here, and you were bleeding half to death in the truck, I saw Samuel among the other men. Clean-shaven, he would have been impossible to miss. That's probably why I recognized him at all. If I'd had time to think about it, I would have realized what an outrage it would seem to him. I left swearing on everything holy that I would never marry, and when I came back—" She didn't finish. She knew J.D. understood her well enough. "He's aged terribly—"

J.D. cut her off with one of those smoldering looks alone. A look that meant he considered her his territory. He touched her cheek, and she flinched, wanting it so bad, fearing it even more. Pleasure coursed down her spine and she shivered. "He had to have been too old for you to marry anyway."

She agreed that he was, but she kept locked in her heart that it was because Samuel was so old and widowed that he had agreed to take her without complaint of all her sins.

J.D. stroked her lower lip with his thumb. His intensity, more familiar to her now, still frightened her. Or maybe it was the force of her own feelings, the places in her soul where she had no forgiveness for herself, that scared her so badly.

He kept pulling her back from that abyss of her past, pulled back her scarf and cradled her neck in his hand, pulling her more with his eyes into his kiss. Their lips touched, just…touched. She exhaled sharply. She had no defenses left her, no hope of stemming her own desire.

She wanted to want him.

His lips moved against hers. "Annie Thorne, I'm glad you refused him." Then he pressed his mouth to hers, his tongue into hers to forestall her protesting his calling her by his last name, but she sank so deeply, so suddenly, so irreversibly into wanting him, into needing what he gave her, into *him* that she would never have found the words and never uttered them if she had.

She found herself returning the silky, erotic caresses of his tongue, the searching of his lips. The scrape of his whiskers on her neck aroused a feverishness in her that at last she had to break off their kiss or die for wanting too much more. She rested her forehead against his, and the only sound in the dark and hay-scented barn was the ragged neediness of their breathing.

AT HALF PAST TEN at night, Andreas drove one of the colony's extended cab pickups into the yard. Ann bundled up and followed J.D. out of the bookbinder's hut. Edgy and simmering, Timothy barged out the door of his apartment, followed by a woman in a down-filled comforter whom Ann thought must be Andreas's wife. Timothy didn't even bother to send her packing back inside.

Andreas had hopped out of his side and opened the passenger door. Samuel fell drunk to the frozen ground, muttering hellfire and damnation on the lot of them.

The woman flew to Andreas's side. He put an arm around her, silently conveying his well-being. "Ann, J.D., I'm really sorry."

Holding her around the shoulders as well, J.D. grimaced. "What happened?"

"I drove straight into town and checked out all the bars, but Samuel wasn't anywhere around. He had a head start on me, but not that much. I guessed he must have hitched a ride into Great Falls, so I headed there. By the time I scoured the bars there and got back to Cold Springs and found him, he was drunk as a skunk, talking his fool head off to anyone who would listen."

Timothy called upon God to forgive Samuel, as no one else was likely. "Andreas, help me carry him. Mary, you go on ahead and prepare Samuel's bed. Ann, take your husband and get some sleep."

Mary parted from her husband and moved silently away, but Andreas planted his feet, his body language firm. "I'm going to need to talk to Ann and J.D., Timothy."

"There's no need of talk, talk, talk," Timothy snapped. "Whatever talking needs to be done, I will do in the morning."

Andreas cleared his throat. The freezing cold, perhaps fear of things thus far unsaid, sent a powerful shudder through his lean body. He stuck his hands deep in his coat pockets. "Timothy, this is not a good situation. It might help them—" he angled his elbow toward Ann and J.D. "—to hear about what I saw."

Timothy stood staring in frozen disbelief at his brother's obstinacy. Exhaling streams of frustration, he shook his head and bent over to haul Samuel up by the shoulders. Andreas stuck a powerful arm beneath Samuel's knees and lifted. Mary had gone ahead to open the door to the apartment where Samuel lived with his married sister and her family.

Watching them cart the drunken man away, J.D. shivered hard. Her nerves stretched already to the breaking point, Ann took his arm. "Go back inside. I'll make us some coffee." When he resisted moving, seemed not even to have heard her, she grew alarmed. "J.D., go back inside, please. You'll wear yourself out and relapse and we don't need that."

Her urgency must have broken through to him. He gave a short nod, turned and trudged back over the frozen, snowpacked earth.

She went to the kitchen, expecting only to find an industrial-size percolator, but came upon a small six-cup coffeemaker. It took several minutes, and Andreas was already sitting with J.D. in the bookbinder's hut, deep in conversation when she arrived with the pot and three mugs.

Andreas blessed her, and wrapped his cold fingers around the mug. J.D. took his mug in hand and for lack of a third chair, guided her to sit on his right leg.

She felt a warm flush on her cheeks, but Andreas showed no embarrassment at all over the intimacy, just swallowed coffee. "I was just saying I didn't get in on much of whatever venom Samuel poured out. I wasn't there in time. He was already three sheets to the wind when I got there. Point is, J.D., your name came up."

J.D.'s hand closed fist-tight around the fabric of her dress. Ann took the blame. "I can't believe I didn't think further ahead than that! It would have been so simple to make up a name before we got here."

Despite his anxiety, J.D. refused to let her heap the heat on herself. "Give yourself some credit, Ann. You came here in the first place because you had no reason to believe anything like this would ever happen. Andreas, did you get the impression that anyone in particular was interested in what Samuel had to say?"

Her brother sighed heavily, his forehead creasing in concentration. "It's hard to say. The yokels in town all think it's hilarious to get one of us liquored up. It's just sport with them."

"Any strangers?" J.D. pressed. "Anyone you know is involved in the TruthSayers?"

Again, Andreas didn't know. "We don't frequent the bars, so there's no way I would know everyone. I recognized a couple of local hell-raisers, but they must have been bored with him by the time I got there. I don't personally know any TruthSayers. We just hear a lot of rumors. We hear they are everywhere. Eyes and ears, you know?

"Anyway, Samuel couldn't have had enough money on him to buy two beers, let alone get himself soused, so someone was footing the bill. Maybe for the entertainment value or maybe to pump him for whatever he knew."

J.D. sat silent, thoughtful for a moment. His hand rubbed small circles in the small of her back. The repetitive motion probably eased his tension as much as it eased her own anxiety.

She knew it was impossible to expect Andreas to have noticed the kinds of things in the bar that she or J.D. would have picked up by second nature. Who sat quietly listening, who got up when, who egged Samuel on, who tried to hush him up. Andreas had to be questioned as they would a civilian witness.

She asked those kinds of questions until her brother volunteered that there had been some sort of weird competition going on in the few minutes he'd observed Samuel before he'd gone in and pried him loose.

"Competition?" she repeated.

"Yeah. One guy'd ask some idiot question just to get Samuel riled up, and this other guy'd interrupt, like he was trying to get the attention for himself."

"Can you describe them?" J.D. asked.

"Maybe. The guy with the idiot questions was about six feet, weighed maybe two-ten. Light brown hair, ruddy complexion. I'd have thought he was your typical farmer, but he was wearing those khaki pants and some real nice silk shirt."

"And the other one?"

"He was dark-haired, I'd even say it was black. Couple days' growth of a beard. Lean, mean-looking kind of guy like you see in the movies, only this guy was a real sad sack, crying in his beer worse than Samuel."

J.D. nodded, but she knew by his level concentration that the descriptions were as meaningless to him as they were to her. What really mattered was that there were men present in that bar listening to Samuel carrying on—and that J.D.'s name was out there.

She turned slightly on his leg, toward him. "Do you think we should try to leave tonight?"

J.D. sighed heavily. Andreas started shaking his head. "Look, it's up to you guys what you do. But it seems to me that if there were TruthSayers in that bar, they'll be just waiting for you to hit the road."

"Timothy is right, the colony is in danger now," Ann protested. "We can't stay here indefinitely, Andreas."

"Timothy would pitch a real fit, now, wouldn't he?" Her brother grinned. "Sure you don't want to join up with the brethren, J.D.? It's not a bad life."

Despite their fairly nasty situation, J.D. laughed. "That'd be a real match. I'm an undercover cop. Played a priest once for a couple of months. I could probably hack it." He pinched Ann on the bottom. "What do you say, sweetheart? Shall we just forget all this and stay?"

She couldn't even reach his hand to slap it. "Very funny. Both of you. A laugh a minute. Suppose you two comedians come up with a way to get us out of here."

"I don't know," J.D. drawled. "I'm kinda liking

the lifestyle. Little woman taking care of me. Kinda grows on a guy, ya know?''

She gave him a look, then turned sweetly to Andreas. "You're what? Thirty-seven now?''

"January fourth.''

"And how many babies do you and Mary have?''

He got her drift and gave a sly grin. "Twelve. Working real hard on a baker's dozen.''

J.D. turned a little green.

"Wouldn't that be fun, J.D.?'' She pouted. "But I bet you'd miss that sweet little lime-green Camaro—''

"Whoa, wait. Not even. Get up, wench, you're making my leg fall asleep.''

"Dream on.''

Andreas fell half off his chair laughing.

She did leave J.D.'s lap. She could feel his leg trembling, knew he was tiring.

"It might liven things up around here if you guys stayed,'' Andreas said, sobering up. "But I do have a suggestion.''

"Yeah?'' J.D. clearly liked this brother a lot.

"Say you wait till tomorrow night. There isn't going to be anytime that's safe for you to leave by the main roads, but we've got this wagon that we have sleigh runners for.

"It takes a little time to change things out,'' he went on, "but then we can hitch up a couple of horses around nightfall, and take you cross-country to Walden. Do you remember it, Annie? Hardly bigger than a post office, but the old guy there used to give us ice cream when he bought all that corn.''

"Oh, wow! Yes. I do remember him.''

"And what would be the point of getting to Walden?" J.D. asked.

"A sleigh ride, of course," Andreas cracked, leaning forward, elbows on his knees. "No, really. Friday nights around eleven o'clock, a bus goes through all the way to Billings. Another one comes by headed north about an hour later. Anybody waiting there, the driver stops. Other than that, the place is dead. There's no way anyone could anticipate you doing that. Plus, you see anyone who sees you."

J.D. gave a low whistle of appreciation. "Works for me. Ann?"

"It's brilliant, Andreas."

He sat back, well nigh pleased with himself. "We don't get much opportunity to be real innovative around here. I thought about this driving back with Samuel puking his guts out every couple of miles. Gave me something to think about besides dumping the sorry sack on the side of the road." His expression grew serious again. "Annie, I'm sorry for all your trouble. Sorrier we're the cause of any of it."

A frown creased J.D.'s forehead. He shook his head in confusion. "You're not the cause of anything."

"We just think like that, J.D.," Andreas explained. "Probably something you should understand about my baby sister, if you don't already. See, from the time we're knee high to a grasshopper that's what we're taught. Always look for blame in ourselves first. The old mote-in-the-eye thing." He winked at Ann. "Especially if you're a girl."

Tears welled up in her eyes. "Oh, God, Andreas, I have missed you! I didn't even realize how much."

He rolled his eyes at her, but he was as quick to

his feet as she was to give her a real hug. "I wish you were here, sweatpea. Place is kinda dull without you."

A part of her so longed for her place where she had never fit in, always been the ugly duckling, that she had to turn away. She looked at J.D. "We also have the money problem. I had a stash in the Honda, but I gave it to Manny, and—"

J.D. swore softly. They'd been through this before, but now the solution shook free in his muddled brain. "I don't know where my head is. Garrett, Matt and I all have a credit card issued under the same false identity. There's a fifty-thousand-dollar limit, but the point of having it was always to be able to track each other if something like this ever happened."

Ann smiled, half in relief of evidence that his memory seemed a little better all the time, half for the beauty of the scheme, its utter simplicity. "So if one of you is using the credit card, the other two are notified?"

"Yeah." J.D. nodded. "Or if one of us has been knocked out of the game and the card stolen. Whatever, the other two of us would always have a jump on what's going down."

Andreas grinned. "Like bread crumbs. I love it."

"I'd have loved it a lot more if I'd remembered before this." He shook his head. "So, it's a plan, then?" J.D. asked.

"It's a plan." Andreas stuck out his hand and J.D. met his grip. "I want to say this in case I don't get a chance again." His expression became admiring. "If Annie was going to break her own rule and get herself married, she did it right."

ANDREAS LEFT. J.D. made short, unselfconscious work of stripping down to his boxers. He lay down under the sheet and comforter, and watched Ann taking down her hair, berating himself for forgetting until now the credit-card gambit. He'd had a concussion. Fine. But this kind of stuff had come second nature too many years to find it excusable.

His head had ached so long, throbbed so constantly, that he was by now operating in spite of it. Through it, somehow. But the injuries were still taking a toll in weakness to which he wasn't accustomed, and a level of exhaustion he knew he'd been to before but couldn't remember.

Well, he couldn't remember anything important at the moment, anything that mattered, now, could he?

And then there was the emotional component. He needed Ann. Wanted her. He'd wanted to tease her, to say to her after Andreas's parting remark that this marriage really ought to be consummated sometime soon.

He could take a joke about a baker's-dozen babies. He couldn't joke about consummating anything with her because it wouldn't really be a joke at all.

Not to him.

She had slept on this same bed with him every night, but she slept on top of his covers and pulled the edges back over to cover herself.

Ah, God.

He would watch her each morning, braiding her hair, twisting strands one beneath, one over. To see her deft fingers accomplishing their sullen goal was what he imagined it must be to see the outcry of a poem in its construction. He wasn't given to thinking in such terms, didn't even know he really knew the words, but he would think he wished sincerely to be couplets in her hands, uncoupled, stanzas to be wrought.

Her unwitting sensuality in the braiding of her hair reminded him sharply, painfully, of her tongue touching his neck, or her lips touching his, her hand in his atop the covers, cradling his hardened flesh.

Now he watched her beautiful, slender fingers moving through the braids, teasing them apart. His eyes could barely stay open at all, but to watch her fingers stripping order from her hair was to want her unraveled completely in his arms, in his heart and in his mind.

He could not take his eyes from the simple feminine task of undoing what she had done to make herself less an object of a man's lust.

No doubt feeling the force of his attention to her every move, she looked up at him. She drew an unsteady breath, forgot to let it go. "Thorne?"

He thought to ask her, would she come under the covers with him? But he was either afraid of her answer or the exhaustion took its final toll of the day. He fell asleep before he could even think to protest.

Chapter Eight

He dreamed that night that he lay in the arms of a flame-haired angel. His body thought otherwise. He shifted uneasily in his sleep all night long. Ann dozed on and off, but his discomfort kept her awake most of the night.

An hour before dawn he woke, every part of him aching. It was as if his body had reserved the extent of the aches and pains until his head and bullet wound had begun to heal. But he'd been slammed hard in the chest, and thrown back hard in the confines of the telephone booth. There wasn't a part of him that wasn't protesting now.

Ann got up in the dark with only the scant light of the moon filtering in through the curtains to get him some aspirin. "Would you like a hot mineral bath?"

He raised himself up on one elbow, swallowed the pills and some water. "I would kill for a hot bath."

She sat beside him in her thin flannel nightgown, stroking his hair as he lay back down. "It's a communal bathhouse, but no one will bother us. Baths around here are usually Saturdays. Do you mind that, or—"

He grimaced a little. "Only the trip through the Antarctic to get there."

"Well, then. You shall have a nice long soak." She smiled tenderly at him. "There's a water heater now. It shouldn't take me too long to run your water. I'll come get you." She started to stand. He caught her wrist and drew her back into his arms for a kiss, unable to imagine why the scent of her alone, or the feel of her unbound breasts against him wasn't enough to cure him of every ill.

She stayed in the kiss longer than he dared hope. He knew the colony bell would clang soon and she would have to dress and deal with her hair lest someone accidentally see her breaking Timothy's rules.

She dressed out of his sight, bound up her hair without the mandatory braids, put on the heavy down coat her brother had brought her and slipped out into the dark.

He got up and dressed for the cold as well, and when she returned for him, followed her back to the bathhouse. Half a dozen old-fashioned claw-footed tubs, retrofitted for modern plumbing more with functionality than beauty in mind, sat all in a row in the light of the oil lantern from the bookbinder's hut.

Steam rose off the one she had filled for him, coating the small windows. Stripping quickly, he nearly groaned in anticipation.

Ann sat on the side of the tub, busying herself casting small handfuls of mineral salts into the water, but the intimacy of it all worked against her studied and casual indifference.

The low light of the lantern cast a small golden glow in the darkness.

The space meant for many saved all to her and Thorne.

The steam, the haze, the heat, his body, battered and bruised and aching, still so powerfully built, all of it came together to saturate her senses, to steep her in the knowledge of her own desire. Awareness she had kept so silent and so still for so long would no longer play dead.

This was the lust and awareness of herself and of what she wanted that the whole of the Cold Springs colony could never discipline out of her. This was her sin, her carnal nature, which she could not believe was bad or evil, only the fulfillment of all that was good and wonderful between a man and a woman.

She dared not breathe, could not keep her eyes off his body, off the long lean muscles of his haunches, or the bone or sinew or shadowed sex. A living, breathing master sculpture of a man.

In her dreams, she knew, this hauntingly chaste, sexual moment would return to her again and again.

She had never thought of her bed as lonely. Now she would never think otherwise. But the loneliness would always serve to remind her that her freedom was much too precious to be bartered away for so fleeting a thing as desire.

She stirred herself out of her fog. He stepped into the tub and sank down in the water till the level rose to his neck, then farther still, till his knees poked out and his head was covered and the stinging heat bathed the knot on his head.

When he came up for air, a slow, grateful smile formed on his lips. His eyes stayed closed. ''I think I've died and gone to heaven.''

"Doesn't get much better, does it?"

"Mmm."

She wanted to stay, needed to go. "I'll come back in a little while. If it cools off too much—"

"Stay."

"J.D.—"

"Please." His eyes opened, though in the darkness she could hardly see what was expressed there. "Ann." His beautiful deep voice was thick, scratchy with the same overwhelming desire that was thick in her. "I've fallen in love with you, Annie Thorne. Just thought you should know."

Seconds passed, still she couldn't breathe. She felt at once hot and shivering, at the same time panicked and profoundly excited, frozen and never more alive. He smiled, watching the play of emotions through her, and then sank below the surface again and emerged with a shiftless grin. "Besides, every time you leave me alone, I get into trouble."

He stole through her every defense. She could only scold. "You do have a knack for that," she agreed. "I—" She broke off, listening hard. There was something going on outside, maybe the older boys going out to get a few chores done before breakfast. She didn't want to alarm J.D. but she felt uneasy. "I'll stay. You just rest there and let the hot water work on you."

He nodded and let himself relax again. She stood and moved to the windows, wiping a small circle to see through the steam, cracking open one of the windows a very little bit. The movement of the boys seemed oddly urgent. Timothy appeared briefly at a knock on his door, sending them all back inside.

At last she saw what the commotion was about,

and the bottom dropped out of the pit of her stomach. Two sedans and at least one, maybe two four-wheel-drive utility vans turned silently and without headlights in the dark from the road leading into the colony to the very center of the buildings. Still silent, all four turned on the flashing red beacons, and the one in the lead its floodlights.

Her heart knocked hard, too slow inside her. She glanced at J.D. and knew that he had picked up on her uneasiness before the silently ominous red lights began to flash through the night.

He never moved. Not a ripple. He was never more calm or disciplined than when a situation tilted out of control or reached a desperate, crisis level.

"Thorne, I don't know what Timothy will do—"

"Even if he turns us over, they're not going to shoot me in front of a hundred or more witnesses." His voice was so low she could barely hear him. "Talk to me. Tell me what's going on."

She swallowed hard. The unlikely had happened. It didn't matter whether there had been one or a dozen TruthSayers sitting around in that bar last night. It didn't matter whether one or several had gathered in Cold Springs because Martin Rand had betrayed J.D., or only unwittingly given away what he knew, or if Rand had himself been betrayed trying to help them. In any case, it was Samuel who had blown their safe haven wide open.

J.D. lay back in the claw-footed tub, knowing there was absolutely nothing he could do to save himself, or that she could do either. They could only wait and see what happened.

She took his advice and simply reported what she saw, describing six men piling out of four vehicles without any unnecessary show of force or guns. In the crisp, frozen air of the foothills, the sound of voices came clearly through the window she had cracked open.

"Timothy Tschetter! This is Sheriff Sinclair. Can we talk?"

"He's coming out," Ann whispered. Her brother had opened the door of his apartment, shrugging into his coat as he trudged heavily down the stairs, saying nothing until he approached the half-dozen men. In his understated way, Timothy went on the offensive.

"Haven't seen this kind of thing happen in forty years, Sheriff. Hope I don't see it again in my lifetime."

"Now, don't go jumping to conclusions, Timothy. This isn't trouble—"

"No," Timothy agreed equably. "This is an outrage. Coming upon us before the sun is even up, like thieves in the night."

"This is nothing like that. Just take it easy. Got a man here needs to talk to you real bad, and that's all there is to it." He jabbed a finger to his left, pointing at the man beside him in a long black overcoat. "We've come at the request of a United States marshal, Timothy, and I'd consider it a personal favor if you'd just talk to the man."

Ann exchanged looks with J.D. in the low light of the oil lantern. The presence of a federal marshal smacked of Rand's intervention. The possibility cracked open that Samuel Pullman wasn't the only one who'd betrayed them. The kindest interpretation of the facts was that Rand had taken matters into his own hands, disregarding J.D.'s explicit refusal of protective custody. The only alternatives were that Rand was himself a TruthSayer or an unwitting dupe.

Rand had never been unwitting in his life.

In a single, soundless motion, J.D. rose from the tub of water and began to dry himself.

The marshal stepped forward and introduced himself. "Mr. Tschetter, my name is Carson. Sandy Carson." Ann sent J.D. another look. He didn't recognize the name either. "I apologize for the inconvenience, sir," Carson was saying. "We have come to take J. D. Thorne and Ann Calder into protective custody. This is purely a rescue operation, for their benefit. We chose this unpleasant hour because we wanted to be sure our movements didn't raise any untoward interest, so—"

"What kind of interests would untoward ones be?" Timothy asked, interrupting, at once seeming either too dense to be dealt with or too smart to be taken in.

Sinclair frowned. "Timothy? Did you understand—"

"Have you ever known me to fail to understand what's been said to me?" Timothy asked.

"No. So, well, then—"

"I can't help you."

"Can't, Timothy, or won't?" a younger deputy asked.

Ann watched, describing to J.D. the scene as Timothy turned to address the insolence. "Sheriff Sinclair and I go way back. We are, or up until this moment, have been friends who call each other by name. To you, I am Mr. Tschetter."

The federal marshal and Sinclair spoke at once to mitigate the rudeness, then Sinclair deferred.

"Mr. Tschetter, this not an arrest, and no one here is in any trouble. All I ask is that you let Mr. Thorne and Ms. Calder know that we are here, offering protection."

But Timothy only repeated himself. "I can't help you."

Ann fended off a terrible shiver. "If this is a standoff with Timothy," she uttered softly, "they lose."

"Temporarily." J.D. didn't think they'd let it go at that. He pulled on the fresh clothes Andreas had given him. "Someone's going to be embarrassed if they don't come away with us now."

"Timothy, now listen to me," the sheriff said, "because we are old friends and we go back a long way. You know Samuel was in town last night and he let slip more than their names. J. D. Thorne and Detective Ann Calder are here. Leastwise, I'm figuring Annie Tschetter and the detective are the same since Samuel was so up in arms. Wouldn't that be your baby sister, now, Timothy?"

Timothy shrugged. "She's been gone a very long time now. Besides, there's no accounting for what gets Samuel up in arms. If there are any damages to be paid, we'll pay them. If you want to take him off to your jail cells, you have my blessing. Samuel Pullman no longer knows what he's talking about."

Dressed now, approaching the window, J.D. shivered. "Does he mean that?"

"No. It's a bluff, but Sinclair has no way of knowing that," she whispered back.

The marshal spoke again. "This isn't a matter of damages, sir, or of what one of your flock knows or doesn't know. We know Thorne and Calder are here. If they believe that they're safe here with you, well, then, we'll drive on out of here same way we came in." Same game, Ann thought, a bluff. The marshal had no intention of leaving without them. Next he would put the fear of God into Timothy.

"Sir, we believe they are in grave danger. Injured, without the resources to protect themselves, or your entire colony for that matter, when—not if—matters come to a head."

Timothy stoically repeated himself once more. "I can't help you."

"Suppose we help ourselves then. Just take a look around?" the sheriff barked. "Is that the way you want this to go?"

"I would have to see a court order," Timothy replied. "Do you have one?"

"Mr. Tschetter," the marshal complained, "we're here to offer protection, not to search your premises."

Unhappy with his failure, the sheriff grew peevish. "Suppose we call all your people out here—"

"That," Timothy agreed, "I would be happy to do for you."

Ann clapped a hand over her mouth. What could he be thinking? J.D. pulled her into his arms and they both stood there, leaning against the wall not more than thirty feet from a handful of lawmen.

The marshal accepted the offer. Timothy went to the colony bell and summoned the entire populace with three quick peals of sound that died sudden deaths in the vast outdoors.

Peering through the cracked window space, Ann watched as families began streaming silently out of their apartments, men, women, children of every size and age spreading out in a large solemn circle that finally enclosed the searchlights. She could no longer see Timothy or any of the six lawmen.

The sheriff must have made a careful survey of the adult men. "I don't see Samuel Pullman here, Timothy."

Her brother replied, but it was far more difficult now, with everyone grouped around, to hear what was said.

J.D. let her go so he could watch as well from the other side of the window. A couple of big, husky teenagers broke free of the circle. "Do you know what's going on?"

She shrugged. "Those boys are going toward Samuel's sister's apartment. Timothy probably told him to go get Samuel."

"In the meantime," the sheriff's shout went up, "I would like to ask the rest of you to tell us where we can find J. D. Thorne and Ann Calder, whom you know as Annie Tschetter. We're here to help them. We're here to spare your colony acts of violence because you have given them a place to hide." He began, Ann thought, to go around the circle, looking for familiar faces, calling out the names of men he knew. "Andrew Wurz?" Silence. "John Kleinsasser?"

Each name called met with an almost eerie silence. Ann hugged her waist. Tears welled up in her eyes for the loyalty of good people on whom she had turned her back. A few of the littlest children began to cry from the cold and tension-riddled dawn.

J.D. drew a harsh breath. "That's it, Ann. I'm not going to hide behind women and babies."

He brushed past her, but she grabbed his biceps. "If you go out there now, J.D.," she whispered, "they will have done all this for nothing. Please." Her heart felt stuck high in her throat for what he was willing to sacrifice to spare the colony, but he could not undo this any more than he was responsible for or could undo anything she had done.

He shook his head. "It doesn't matter. Samuel will blow this wide open."

"Timothy can handle Samuel or he would never have sent for him."

"He had no choice, Ann."

"Wait and see. Please. Don't make what they're doing for us meaningless."

The sheriff ran out of names he knew. He began asking random children. "You, little girl..." "Son, what about you?" J.D. stood rigidly listening, his jaw clenched, tension and anger like sparks flying off him that women and children would be dragged out of their homes in the subzero cold before dawn and interrogated on his account.

At last Samuel came stumbling down his sister's stairs. The circle came apart to admit him. Ann could only see him for a brief instant before he disappeared into the circle. He looked fearful, defiant.

Timothy called loudly. "Samuel Pullman wishes to apologize for his drunken, sinful behavior in town last night."

In her mind's eye, Ann saw herself where Samuel now stood. She knew this kind of collective wrath, this pressure, the coercion to bend, to become one with the community of believers who together represented the will of the Almighty.

Samuel was not strong enough to hold up against it; he would acquiesce and keep the silence. The sheriff got nothing from Samuel but an apology for his foray into their world, where sin was not sin and shame was not shame, none save Samuel's own. He got drunk and he bore false witness against his neighbors, and even when he was asked directly about Ann or J.D., about the things he had said the night before in front of so many witnesses, Samuel had nothing to say at all.

The colony, down to the smallest child, held their tongues. For all his willingness to put a stop to the charade and turn himself in, J.D. sank against the wall of the bathhouse with relief. Ann continued watching while the circle of believers began to drift away, and finally the sheriff and marshal and their various underlings were left alone again with her brother.

"This is a mistake, Timothy," the sheriff warned. "These folks you're harboring—your *sister*—is in a heck of a lot of danger, and you're not doing the colony any favor in that regard either. I don't think you understand the kind of men—"

"Who would kill another man? You're right. But the Lord works in mysterious ways," Timothy said. "You see, we expect suffering here on earth. And adversity always brings us more firmly together in the Lord than before."

BY NOON the wagon had been converted with sled runners into a sleigh, but the plan to take them out could not be moved up. There was no way they could move across the landscape without being seen in the daylight, nor would any buses pass by before late into the night. But to J.D.'s everlasting amazement, the early-morning incursion of the cops left the people in the colony more cohesive and less anxious than before, almost giddy. Whatever threat there may be of the sheriff returning before day's end with the necessary papers to conduct a search simply amused them. Ann thought it played into the colony's ingrained us-against-them mentality. The world encroaching in such a manner was just more reinforcement to them that their lifestyle was necessary and justified.

A couple of times low-flying airplanes passed overhead that Timothy had never seen before. Men like Timothy, who lived their lives outdoors, who made their living by the sweat of their brows, were also men who noticed such things.

It took no leap of imagination to surmise that someone was doing aerial reconnaissance, and that *someone* was unlikely to be local law enforcement. No judge was going to authorize a warrant for the search of a colony. No crime had been committed by Ann or J.D., nor was it a crime to give them sanctuary.

If it weren't for the aerial surveillance, J.D. could almost have believed that he had lost all sense of proportion. He and Ann might have been not only well advised but perfectly safe in the custody of the federal marshal. J.D. just wasn't ready to bet their lives on it.

It was a physical and practical impossibility for there to be TruthSayers present in all places at all times. With Chet Loehman murdered at the hands of Ross Vorees, and Vorees already sentenced to life without parole in Wyoming, the leaderless Truth-Sayers should have been reduced to a shambles, nothing more than a motley collection of like-minded law-and-order fanatics with no common agenda.

But in all the months J.D. had worked to uncover the clandestine vigilantes remaining in the ranks of legitimate law enforcement, he'd given them a rallying point himself.

J. D. Thorne had become the common enemy.

He tried to talk it through with Ann over their noon meal because there were just too many variables to penetrate.

She carved a bit of chicken from the thighbone. "I don't believe the visit this morning from the sheriff and federal marshal proves anything, Thorne. By their account, Sinclair and the marshal, Carson, knew we were here in the colony because of Samuel's drunken talk. There was no mention of Rand. If he had decided to send in the feds over your refusal of protective custody, wouldn't Rand still have made sure the marshal mentioned his name, expecting that you'd be persuaded it was safe to go with them?"

"Yeah, he probably would," J.D. conceded. On his plate now was only a pile of bones. He set it aside.

"And the other thing I've been thinking about," Ann went on, "is that we have no proof the TruthSayers have been involved at all." All it would have taken, she reasoned, was ordinary Montana cops sitting in the bar with Samuel, alert to the news out of Seattle of the attempt on J.D.'s life.

He had to admit the possibility. "The only problem is that the sheriff and marshal were here inside of eight or ten hours. That just doesn't happen without some serious coordination."

Ann nodded. Ordinary cops would probably have given Samuel a lift back to the colony, and as fellow cops, warned J.D. immediately that his cover there was blown. The TruthSayers, on the other hand, wanted him dead. Without a detailed understanding of the colony, there would be no way for them even to send in a lone assassin. Forcing them out was the TruthSayers' only option.

The reconnaissance implied a certain measure of organization and determination as well.

J.D. spent the last hours until they could put Andreas's escape plan into action pacing the small bookbinder's hut, combing through those few details of the day he'd been shot that he'd been able to reassemble.

He had watched Ann's testimony on the closed-circuit monitor in his office. He hadn't seen her in months, hadn't been happy about not seeing her either.

He'd gone to Rand's place on Mercer Island. According to Rand, they'd discussed the trial. He had a sense of having been even less happy when he left than when he'd arrived at the Mercer Island estate.

What was it?

He couldn't imagine what had induced him to break his promise to Ann and go to her place, how low he must have been feeling. In his mind, he would have had to have been near hopeless to turn up at her place, but all he had to go on was the unsettling notion echoing itself that Martin Rand had been stringing him along in some way he couldn't even fathom.

He knew all about betrayals. How, come what may, people were inevitably able to justify themselves and their actions. But Rand's name in the same thought with "betrayal" just wouldn't gel. On the other hand, he knew that the failure to bring them out of the colony, whether the TruthSayers had been party to the early-morning inquisition or not, would only provoke the vigilantes to other, more depraved means of flushing him and Ann out of their safe haven.

He would have to call Rand again, from wherever they landed after the night's travels. The only way to know for certain whether Rand was involved with the TruthSayers was to give him information only he could reveal. What that would be, J.D. didn't know.

After the noon meal, Ann went about eliminating all traces of their stay. The point was moot, of course. Everyone and everyone's brother knew she and J.D. were here, but it gave her something constructive to do.

She needed it.

The colony council, composed of seven men including Timothy, the preacher, Andreas, another of Ann's brothers and three other men had been meeting most of the afternoon. In the way of knowing something was afoot among people who lived so closely together, she understood this was no random meeting.

She suspected something was not only amiss, but very wrong for it to take all these men, who spent their entire lives together and in many ways knew each other better than they knew their wives, all afternoon to hash through a decision.

She glanced out the window of the bookbinder's hut, by some uncanny instinct at just the moment the colony council emerged from Timothy's office.

But then the dinner bell rang and the evening meal intervened. As usual, their meal was delivered to the bookbinder's hut. By six o'clock, when darkness had long since fallen, Andreas and his wife, Mary, knocked at the door.

J.D. let them in. The two of them discarded their coats, then moved toward the chairs. Ann and J.D. sat side by side on the bed. Andreas started in, introducing his wife, whom they had already seen the night before.

"Annie, we have to talk. There are things about Samuel that you and J.D. should know."

"It took all day to decide there are things about Samuel that I should know?"

Mary answered softly. In her late thirties, and for having given birth twelve times, she seemed younger, not as worn out as Ann had imagined she must be. "These are complicated things for us to speak of, Ann. Things better forgotten, really, except that they are not…forgotten."

J.D. took her hand and settled it beneath his on his thigh. "I take it the council decided we should know these things?"

Andreas nodded. "Annie…do you want—" He couldn't seem to get it out. He started over. She worried because it felt to her as if Andreas had become suddenly uneasy around J.D. He took a deep breath and plunged ahead. "Years ago, after you ran away, we had no idea, no way of knowing what had become of you—but that was the way of it. We had lost you, and thought…we believed we would never hear of you again. But Samuel left us at about the same time. We believed his pride had gotten between Samuel and the Lord, that he could no longer live here…after what had happened."

"After I had rejected him?" Ann clarified. Andreas and Mary nodded. Still, Ann had no idea where he was headed. "Go on, Andreas."

He sat with his forearms planted on his thighs, his hands around a mug of coffee, his eyes fixed somewhere in the dark brew. "You probably won't remember this. Samuel is seven years older than me, but he had never gone off touring. He just wasn't the type. He fit here. He had no longings for the outside, ever. He was baptized at eighteen."

"Is that rare?" J.D. asked.

Andreas shrugged. "It is early. Most of us don't choose to be baptized until early or even mid-twenties. It's not uncommon to wait until marriage is in the offing."

"So when he left?" Ann prompted her brother.

"When he left, and we thought he could no longer face us, we didn't expect that he would ever come back. Some thought he would go to another colony."

"But he did return."

Again, Andreas nodded. "He did, Annie. About six months after he left. Then, as you know, he could only be received back if he confessed to all his sins out in the world. To be welcomed back into the fold, he must renounce all that again." Andreas swallowed, sighed, looked regretfully at her. "That was when we learned he had gone to Bozeman."

Andreas looked at her as if asking, Shall I stop?

She understood then, in a blinding flash of unreality, that her sitting on the bed she had shared only in name with J.D., was not at the root of Andreas's discomfort. Her life was about to come unraveled here and now.

Andreas had rightly guessed that J.D. knew none of it.

Her hand clenched beneath Thorne's. "Samuel followed me, then?"

"Yes. And then, I guess you would say he spied on you those months in Bozeman. He's a skilled mechanic. He had no trouble finding work, or any trouble, it seems, paying someone to find where you had gone, or…where you lived, who took the…who took care of you. Names, dates, address, Annie. Everything."

When Andreas could not go on for the awkwardness, Mary went on in his stead. "We have always known what became of you, Annie. We were…" Her voice cracked with emotion. "We were so sad. It broke all our hearts. But then these years went by. Summer came again. The sadness began to fade.

"Then you came back and we… Most of us thought, Annie should know that we know. But Timothy had laid down the law that none of us were to speak with you and the council agreed with him."

She felt so cold. Frozen in time, a scared and miserably lonely sixteen-year-old girl unalterably chained to her past, choking on every faulty decision she had ever made. Thorne's hand had left hers resting on his leg, she didn't even know when.

"Why now, then, Andreas?" she asked.

But it was J.D. who read between the thready lines and understood the added peril, J.D. who spoke without looking at her, his tone so leaden that her heart buckled under its weight. "Let me guess. Samuel told everyone in that bar about the baby."

Chapter Nine

Andreas nodded, mistakenly relieved in his assumption that J.D. had already known about her baby. "I don't know how things like this work. I don't know if the men who are after you would do something with that kind of information or not, but—"

An almost physical pain went through her chest as she finally took in what was at stake. J.D. had warned her. The TruthSayers wanted him dead, and they would stop at nothing.

Her son, the precious little baby she'd carried away from this farm, beneath her heart, in her belly fifteen years before, the infant she had given up for adoption to the man and woman who had taken her in, gave J.D.'s enemies all the leverage they needed.

She couldn't guess exactly what they would do with the information that the Zimmers' teenage son was her illegitimate child. Splashing the scandal in the headlines alone would be enough to ruin their lives.

She could barely speak at all. "I...I have to warn the Zimmers."

J.D. rose. "I'll go get Timothy's cell phone."

Her head jerked up. He was not welcome to move

freely about. "Maybe it would be better if Andreas went."

"I'm sure it would be." He cut her protest short, looking hard at her. He worked his ravaged arm into his sheepskin, then the other, his voice low, strained. "On the other hand, it's really a better idea if I walk this off."

Her chin went up, her eyes down, away from the reproach in his, and he walked out the door, closing it with excessive care. Andreas sat back in his chair, blowing off a breath, tears glittering in his wide gray eyes. "Annie, I'm so sorry."

"It's not your fault, Andreas."

Nor, really, was it hers. She would blame herself, but she had warned Thorne more than once. He had no right to ask or expect her to have told him every detail of her leaving—details she had never shared with anyone, not in all her years on the outside.

And whether he thought her despicable for giving up her baby or whether he didn't, even if he was only disappointed that she hadn't seen fit to share the whole truth with him of her running away, then he would have to live with the disappointment she had promised him would arise.

And so would she.

The look he had just given her was the one she had hoped never to see in his eyes, but the defiance she had learned so unnaturally early and so well crowded her misery.

It didn't matter that her heart was breaking for what might have been between them if she had only been a different woman. If she were the kind of woman who didn't know, who hadn't learned that she could have her freedom, or she could have love, but she could not have both.

It didn't matter that she loved him, or that she had known she loved him months ago, when he had risked everything to save his best friend's life, restoring Garrett to Kirsten, and the two of them back to their son.

So long as you wanted anything, you could never be free.

None of it mattered. She had warned him.

She had warned herself too many times to count.

But Andreas and Mary were truly innocent bystanders, ignorant even of the fact that Thorne was not really her husband. "Please don't blame yourselves. All of this is my fault." If she hadn't come here, if J.D. hadn't come to her, if he hadn't been shot…but he had.

And now it was her own innocent, unwitting child who would suffer.

Having said all that needed to be said, Mary and Andreas stood and gave her fierce hugs, then bundled up again. Andreas turned back at the door. "There's no point in starting out too early. You'll only have to stand outside in Walden waiting on the bus, and freeze to death. I'll have the horses hitched up to the sleigh and ready to go at eight o'clock."

She stood a few moments at the door in the bitter cold looking for J.D. When he didn't show up, she went back inside and put on Mary's old winter coat and sturdy, waterproof boots, gloves and a long black woolen scarf, then went looking for him.

She found him leaning against a barn out of the wind, looking high up into the Rockies, his hands buried deep in the pockets of his sheepskin vest.

The moon and stars glowed brilliantly, reflected light glittering off the fields of snow and frozen landscape. Every pine needle shone, every shadow deepened. The brilliance in the dark of night made her wish all the more deeply that she were someone else, not the adult version of little Annie Tschetter who could not have what she wanted and be loved at the same time.

Maybe she could explain it all to him. Maybe he would go away then, learn to stay away from her with a heart only half-broken, and not irreparable.

She stood before him, looking up into his eyes, saying nothing. She was no rookie when it came to dealing with macho men, but in the moon shadows his whiskered jaw caused him to be more male, more powerfully masculine, more threatening to her sensibilities than she knew how to deal with.

An owl hooted, the wind sighed over the forests of pine leading up the foothills to the mountains. Still she heard him swallow, thought of him swallowing bitter disappointment, and then he took her into his arms and she went there. She circled his waist with her arms and lay her head against his broad, bruised, muscled chest.

For comfort.

For a moment's respite.

He rested his cheek on her head, and they stood together like that, just like that for a space in time both too long and too short.

He shifted his weight; she pulled back, standing on her own again. He crammed his hands back into his pockets; she tucked hers under her arms and spoke first. "Will you walk with me a ways?"

He nodded after a couple of indecisive seconds

and stood away from the wall of the barn. She turned and began picking her way around drifts, a hundred yards, maybe more, through a heavily wooded copse. She could hear him behind her, but never turned back. At last, a bit out of breath, she came to a small clearing and a frozen beaver pond surrounded by towering, centuries-old pine trees.

She led the way down into the frozen meadowland, stepped over a fallen tree trunk and brushed away the worst of the snow, then sat facing the iced-over pond. J.D. straddled the trunk beside her.

"Why are we here, Ann?" He sounded more heartbroken than half already, perhaps expecting her to end it with him, close off any and all possibilities between them.

She swallowed. "This is where it happened."

"Where what happened?"

"My ultimate fall from grace. My own personal version of Eden."

"What does that mean?"

She drew a deep breath, tried to imagine how she could make sense to him, then simply plunged ahead. "When I was very little, five or six, we would sit in German school for an hour every morning before the English teacher came. In those days, Micah Wilmes was the German teacher and the assistant preacher. Many, many days, the boys would sit there rolling spitballs while he asked the girls, usually me, 'What was it like in Eden, Peter Annie?'

"'Who was it who took the apples, Peter Annie?'

"'Who was it who told Eve to taste the apples?'

"'Who told her not to?'

"'What would happen, Peter Annie, if she picked the apple anyway?'"

She had not thought of those grueling hours in many years, but her recollections faithfully reproduced in her the glare of emotion, the icy dread, the heat rising in her face. "I knew the answers. I had heard them in kindergarten since I was three. We learn by sheer repetition, not for the knowledge but to shape us." She paused, refocusing. "Eve wanted the knowledge. She wanted to be smart, to know the difference between good and evil, so she disobeyed the Heavenly Father and took the apples anyway. That's what happened here, all those years later. I wanted to—" She broke off.

Tears welled up in her eyes.

How should one explain a girl's budding sexuality to a man she had fallen in love with, a girl who had been taught as well that lust must be extinguished, that sex was only winked at by God for the sake of children in a marriage? "I wanted to know what to do with all those...feelings."

"What happened here, Ann?" J.D. asked, not having to ask with what feelings she was trying to deal. She had left the colony pregnant.

"When I was fifteen, the rancher whose property borders ours was killed in a car accident. He and his wife had three children under five, and she was pregnant again, nearly six months along when it happened. It was in the summer, at the end of harvest.

"Mrs. Murphy's nephew had come to help her, but the work was just so unending that our men and boys did most of the work. I was sent to live with her that summer, to help her with the children and the new baby when he was born."

"So it was with her nephew, then, that you...that the baby...happened?"

She nodded. His voice, his awkwardness with the words, touched her where she had allowed no one to go and seemed to mirror and magnify her own incongruous innocence. How innocent could a girl be who had been present at the births of half a dozen babies?

But she was.

"He was twenty-three. We flirted all that summer. Even the flirting was new to me. I had no experience with it, or with being alone with a boy."

"That was no boy."

"I know. But…the elders had sent me away as punishment for my many transgressions. When you grow up in a colony, to be left alone or sent to be alone seems like the most unendurable punishment. But it wasn't like that for me. I had the Murphy babies to take care of, and Mrs. Murphy to talk to any time of the day or night. And with him…with him, I felt I wasn't just a girl, either."

She searched for a way to communicate to J.D. what fantastical sensations she had felt, how it came to be that she had allowed herself to be seduced, to be taken. "Special, I guess is the word. I felt hot and excited, feverish. When he touched me, I thought, *this* is love. This can't be wrong. Surely I had misunderstood what was wrong and what was right and good and godly, and I thought no one else in the world had ever felt what I was feeling."

Her throat closed. J.D. never touched her but she felt the heat of his emotion. She had been ripe for the picking, a sensual, rebellious child with no more idea of what was going to happen or what the consequences would be than a child in the world who was only five and not fifteen. "We came here on the night before he was to leave. We took off all our clothes and swam and played in the water and then he began to touch me.''

She shrugged. ''Long story short, I let it happen, J.D. I let it happen because I wanted too much to know what those feelings were about.''

He cleared his throat. ''You never saw him again?''

She shook her head. Her toes were numb with the cold. ''He was gone the next day as planned. By the time I left Cold Springs, Mrs. Murphy had sold the ranch and moved away herself.''

J.D. sat silent for a long time, just staring out at the frozen beaver pond. He started several times to say something, only to break off. She waited. She had had her say. At last he found some words, but the disappointment in his voice was what killed her. ''Did you think, Ann, that it would make a difference to me? That it would change what I feel for you?''

''I didn't know how you would feel about it, J.D. It never occurred to me to wonder. I didn't just forget to mention my baby to you. I had no intention of telling you about him. That wasn't even the point.''

''I don't understand.''

Her heart shrank inside her. She had hurt him in some way she didn't completely understand, as much as in the ways she had foreseen. ''I know.''

''I'm serious, Ann.'' His anger was back with her now. ''Do you think you're the only one with a past? Do you think you've got a corner on the market for regrets?''

''No—''

''Then why—''

''Because I've already disappointed you! Don't

you see? You had an expectation of me that I couldn't fulfill! You wanted me to have told you everything when you asked why I left the colony. You wanted me to trust you enough—"

He swore. "Is that too much to ask, Ann? That you would trust me? Have I done or said anything—"

"It's not too much, J.D.," she interrupted, her voice coming apart. "You're entitled to that and to so much more. But for me it was never a matter of trust. It's a matter of letting myself want what you want for us! What I learned from all of that was that what I wanted was a very dangerous thing."

What she wanted now was a very dangerous thing as well. She wanted nothing more than to let the tears well in her heart and spill from her eyes, nothing so much as to turn her care and loving over to J. D. Thorne because no one had ever understood her half as well or wanted her with such honesty and acceptance as he did, as he was showing her even now. But she would only end up leaving him as she had left everyone else she had ever loved, too scared to sacrifice even the smallest part of the freedom that had cost her everything.

"I learned what it was to get what I wanted, and it wasn't a pretty picture."

"It doesn't have to be like that, Ann."

"It *is* like that, don't you see? I had to leave. I could not have stayed, but to leave like that was more awful than anything I could have imagined. And then I gave my son away, and that was even more hideous, but I was afraid that if I kept him, the colony would somehow find out. I thought they would come for him and they would take him away from me and he would grow up as miserable and misunderstood as I had been, and I couldn't let that happen. I would not let that happen.''

A small cry escaped her after all, for what she had so unwittingly done that might have already destroyed her son. ''God only knows what will happen to him now.'' She would not cry, refused to give in to the self-pity. ''Did you get the cell phone?''

He couldn't look at her. ''Not yet.''

''We should go back then.'' She stood. She had to leave this place behind, had to end a conversation that could have no ending to make him happy. ''It must be getting close to time to leave, and I have to call the Zimmers.''

''What's going to happen, Ann?'' he asked, looking up at her, his voice more strained and raw than she had ever heard before. ''Between us. What's going to happen?''

She opened her mouth to say what had to be said but no words would come out.

He stood and he seemed like the age-old pine trees towering above her with his lantern jaw and his heart stripped bare. ''Tell me nothing is going to happen between us, Annie Tschetter, and I will accept it.''

''J.D.—''

''Nothing is going to happen between us.'' He took hold of her shoulders. ''Say the words, Ann.''

Her lips trembled. She meant to repeat the words after him, but she failed to utter a sound, and he drew her to him as he had another frozen night in Wyoming long months ago, and kissed her till he tasted her tears, and then he let her go.

IN THE BOOKBINDER'S HUT, he handed her the phone. She dialed Montana information and asked for the number of John and Edith Zimmer on Meadowlark Lane in Bozeman.

The operator rang the number, but the connection sounded as if the call might have been forwarded. The voice that answered was clipped, impatient, vastly unlike the bookish gentleman who had given her shelter and adopted her infant son.

"Hello."

Her throat seized. It seemed she could say nothing. Something was wrong. "I'm trying to reach John Zimmer."

"Well, this is the Bozeman P.D." J.D. must have seen the color drain from her face. In a split second he was at her side, listening with her, his own emotional turmoil set aside. "This home is a crime scene," came the impatient demanding voice. "Who am I speaking to?"

She spat out her answer by rote. "My name is Ann Calder with the Seattle P.D. What's going on there?"

"Tell you what's going on here," the voice snapped back. "Teenage monster firebombed his own house. Parents are dead. Kid's on the lam. What's your interest, Seattle? What did you say your name was?"

She all but dropped the phone, shaking, untold dismay rolling over her in waves. J.D. took the phone from her trembling hand and steadied her with his injured arm. The shock had hit her as hard and as surely as if she'd been backhanded. His own blood ran cold with fury.

He'd expected a move on the TruthSayers' part, anything to force him and Ann out of hiding, but jaded as he was, this maneuver hit all new lows for depraved indifference on the part of the TruthSayers.

The timing could be no coincidence. They had acted against him through Ann's son with devastating speed and deadly precision.

Nothing was so certain, so calculated as this to make J. D. Thorne in particular stand up and take notice, leave his cover and lash back.

Another fire, another time, 1980s... His best friend's mother dead of hideous burns and smoke inhalation at the age of thirty-five.

He wondered if they knew, how they knew, then wiped the question from his mind. They knew.

Somehow, the TruthSayers always knew.

If he had thought all day long, he could not have come up with a nastier play than this. He saw through his own rage that despite her years on the streets and in the detective bureau, Ann had never seen anything half so vicious as firebombing the home of an innocent couple and pinning the blame on a kid.

Some previously rational voice inside him suggested he slow down, that he might well be jumping to wild-eyed, crazed conclusions.

But no.

He knew them too well, knew the end always justified the TruthSayers' means. They wanted only to restore real justice. Ask them.

His teeth gnashed. He forced an unnatural calm on himself and improvised, carefully. He could not demand answers from the cops on the other end. He would get no cooperation, especially sight unseen and over the phone, if the P.D. on the scene of the crime believed they were about to be preempted or second-guessed.

He sat down with Ann on the bed, holding the cell phone so that she could hear as well, and used the alias matching his credit card. "Bozeman, this is Hank Altman with the sheriff's office up in Shelby. Have you got a lead on the kid yet?"

Suspicion rankled in the cop's voice. "I thought the woman just said Seattle."

Ann fisted her hand and covered her lips. Twice now she'd given their real names when any damn alias would have been infinitely better.

"She did," J.D. acknowledged, "but she's right here in Shelby on other business. We've just been informed of your situation down there—"

"This is one sorry damn sight worse than a situation, Shelby."

"I understand. Here's the deal. Any possibility the kid had access to a car? Any possibility he'll make a run for the Canadian border?"

"Ain't no way this kid got that far north since he torched this place."

"No?"

"No way. Kid's only fifteen, no car. Parents' vehicles are parked outside. We'll get him, though. He's got no way out." The cop on the other end had already made a couple of faulty assumptions but he was talking, and the longer he talked the better the chances of learning something significant.

"Any idea what set the kid off?"

"All accounts, he's been a handful and a half his whole misbegotten life. Spent some time in juvie hall too. Grocer down the street where the kid works says it ain't in him to do something like this, but that's what they say about every kid that goes freakin' hay-wire these days.''

Ann stiffened, whispering to J.D., "I know the grocer he's talking about."

J.D. nodded and gave her a thumbs-up, empathizing over the phone with the cop's assessment of kids. "Ain't it the truth. I won't hold you up. We'll keep an eye out for him, Bozeman. You let us know if there's anything we can do, you hear?"

"Glad of the offer, Shelby." He covered the mouthpiece of the phone, not well, relaying the gist of the call to some superior, then came back on. "We'll get the little bastard, don't you worry about that."

J.D. swore after the cop hung up. "Not if I have anything to do with it."

WITHIN HALF AN HOUR they were gliding through the deep silence of the night over the snow-crusted landscape, Andreas's handling of the horses nothing short of expert. The rhythmic pounding of their hooves gave an eerie urgency to the night, the quality of time passing, precious seconds ticking away for a teenage boy caught up in a deadly unforgiving game of cat and mouse.

Through all their last-minute preparations and goodbyes, Ann had not shed another tear. He had no idea when or if her iron-willed control would splinter, but knowing what he now knew, J.D. had to believe the woman Annie Tschetter had grown up to be would do what she had to do and save the grief and self-recrimination for a time when it wouldn't matter to another living soul.

She mattered to him in a way no woman—no one

at all—had ever mattered to him before. He had begun to believe she wouldn't let him matter to her;
now, despite her attempt to make him give it up, to
make him acknowledge that she would only keep
disappointing him, he knew she was already beyond
the point of no return.

He mattered to her. What was between them—
more than the unsated physical attraction—mattered
to her. He had to put his faith in her failure.

He held her close in his arms so that when he saw
one lone tear stain her cheek, he thought he would
tear up the earth before anyone made her cry again.

He held her closer but forced himself to think of
other things. With the aerial reconnaissance going
on, by midday tomorrow at the latest, the tracks of
the horses and sled leading to Walden would be seen.
Andreas had decided to drop them there and keep
heading west into the national forest.

If their pursuers were smart, and they were, they
wouldn't be fooled for long. At best, J.D. figured,
they would have no more than twelve hours' head
start, and even that would depend entirely on what
Ann would be able to find out from the old grocer,
Roy Burgess.

It would be the best of all worlds if she could
reach the old man before they committed to the bus
headed south. If her son had headed north, they
would lose ground. They had decided the risk involved was too great to try reaching Burgess at either
the small grocery store or his home, but Andreas
wasn't sure there was a functioning pay phone in
Walden.

If there wasn't, they'd continue with the bus south
and east toward Bozeman until they found a town

where a car could be bought without much notice. And then they would find Ann's son. Then J.D.'s enemy, the one among the TruthSayers whom he had finally threatened too closely, whose name or identity he still could not remember, would learn what it was to screw with J. D. Thorne.

The mind-numbing cold took a serious toll on all three of them. By the kink in his neck, J.D. knew for certain that he had fallen asleep for long, bitterly cold stretches of time.

In the end, J.D. told Andreas to turn around and head home, not to bother trying to make a false trail into the national forest. He could not believe anyone would be fooled by the gambit in any case, and Andreas himself was nearing a state of hypothermia. Even if he fell asleep, the horses would return to the colony and Andreas would be safe.

Touching her forehead, brushing back strands of her hair, Andreas begged Ann to be careful and pulled a navy blue ski cap from his coat pocket. "It wouldn't hurt to keep your hair covered up out there, either, sweet pea. The bad guys will see you coming a mile and a half away."

She blinked away her tears, pushed back the inadequate black woolen scarf and covered her hair with his cap. "I love you, Andreas."

He swallowed hard. "And I've always loved you, Annie." He shook hands and exchanged a rough hug with J.D., then climbed aboard the wagon made into a sleigh and urged the horses back into their paces without a backward glance.

Too cold to think straight, Ann let J.D. hustle her along, walking up and down stretches of highway to keep their circulation going. The bus was twenty minutes late, but managed to pull into the next small town only ten minutes behind schedule. Ann tried Burgess's home phone again in the short stop. Again, no answer. The grocer was either not at home, or ducking his calls.

THEY CROWDED TOGETHER in a phone booth along the bus route at eight in the morning. Ann used J.D.'s alias credit card as a calling card and dialed Roy Burgess's married daughter. She had never liked Ann, turned up her nose in the months she'd worked for Burgess before Jason was born, but they had no other option. They couldn't go anywhere near the firebombed Zimmer house or the grocery store. Burgess's daughter answered on the second ring.

"Gloria?"

"Yes. Who's this?"

"Gloria, this is Ann…Annie Tschetter. Do you remember that I worked for your dad—"

"Annie? Nah. You must have the wrong number—"

"Gloria, please don't hang up. I…it was years ago. Sixteen years ago. I lived with the Zimmers. I used to open the store for your dad so he could go fishing."

"Ann… Oh my dear Lord. You were pregnant. John and Edith's boy is…oh my. What that boy has done, he should burn in hell." She went very quiet, then drew a sharp breath. "You! How do you even dare ring me?"

"Gloria, please, please listen to me. I know Jason—"

"Jaz, you mean? That's what the little hood calls

himself, like he's something special instead of the juvenile delinquent he is.''

Ann gripped the phone till her knuckles shone bone-white. Gloria Crane obviously did not share her father's belief that Jason—Jaz—could not have fire-bombed the Zimmers' home. If she tried to tell Gloria that Jaz had been set up, the woman would probably hang up on her. And might anyway, at any moment.

J.D. had heard her strident accusations as well. He cupped Ann's head in his hand and drew her near to whisper in her other ear. ''Tell her you have to catch up with Jaz before he hurts someone else.''

She nodded, repeating the words, then asked, ''Is your dad safe, Gloria?''

''He's gone off the deep end, that's what. Checked into that dump of a motel off the highway out to Clyde Park. What with all those cops hangin' around, the old coot could be haulin' money in hand over fist if he'd have stayed put and kept that store open. Won't even answer the damn phone. Tells the police that kid ain't done nothing, then goes off an' sticks his head in the sand.''

''He won't be bothered there—''

But Gloria wasn't done complaining. ''I've got half a mind to call the state and get the old fool committed. You keep that kid away from him or I'll come after him loaded for bear. I mean that, Annie Tschetter.''

Chapter Ten

She wanted to go through the phone lines at the horrible woman. "I'm sure you do, Gloria. And if you do that, let me—"

"Say goodbye, Ann," J.D. warned her quietly. "Don't give her any excuse to move on her dad before we can get to him."

She nodded, angrily backhanding a tear from her cheek. "I'm sure your dad will be fine, Gloria. I've been hearing the police believe Jaz hopped a bus to Billings. I just wanted to make sure you were okay. Goodbye."

She hung up the phone and turned into J.D.'s arms, leaning into his chest. In the worst hours of her life, she had never felt so raw, so exposed as this. Her throat made awful, choking sounds. She started shaking and couldn't stop.

He folded her into his arms, and stroked her hair. "Ann, we're going to find Jaz. I promise you, we'll find him. You've just got to keep it together a while longer."

She straightened, nodding, fighting that choked sensation. If she had never left the colony, nothing like this would ever have happened to Jaz, but she couldn't crumble into her own guilt now. "Don't worry about me."

"That's my girl." He kissed her forehead and helped her back onto the bus. By the time they reached the next town it would be nearly nine o'clock, and they could try to find a car for sale.

They got off the bus for the last time half an hour later. J.D. trotted across the small main street to what looked like a community bulletin board outside the packaged-liquor store. Ann took off her knit cap, dragged a hand through the tangle of her hair and then put the ski cap back on and crossed over to join him when he signaled a possibility.

There was only one vehicle in town for sale, an eighties vintage Jeep. The ad said it could be seen parked on the corner of Third and E streets.

The seven blocks took them five minutes to walk. The body of the Jeep was little more than a rust bucket, but the tires were in decent shape. J.D. opened the door and honked the horn. An overweight, heavily jowled man somewhere in his forties ambled out the broken screen door of a very small house.

"Yeah, yeah, yeah. You buyin' or lookin'?"

"Does it run?"

He struggled down three shallow stairs. "Ride's a little rough, but it'll take you anywhere you're going."

"Then I'm buying, but I'm not in any mood to haggle. Give me your best price and we'll see if we've got a deal."

"Five hundred and it's yours."

"Done." He peeled off the five hundred from the thousand Andreas had given him. "Keys?"

The owner drew a key ring out of his pocket and tossed it to J.D., then opened the passenger door, grabbed a ratty-looking title from under the floor mat and signed it over in a cramped hand to J.D.'s alias, Hank Altman.

THERE WERE TEN ROOMS in the motel on the highway headed north toward Clyde Park. J.D. rented one of them, turned over his newfangled Altman credit card and signed them in on an old-fashioned guest register as Mr. and Mrs. Hank Altman, schmoozing with the proprietor about her looking just like that woman who played John Wayne's love interest in *Rooster Cogburn.* "Who was that? Barbara Stanwyck? Kate Hepburn?"

The crusty, birdlike proprietor preened. Ann had to bite her tongue.

There was no one else signed in under the last three days, but she'd noticed as they entered the small, unkempt reception area that the curtains were drawn on all the rooms except cabin nine, and though the keys were hung nearly out of sight, the next to last key was missing as well. With any luck, cabin nine belonged to Roy Burgess. The woman handed J.D. the key to cabin two.

Ann asked politely if they couldn't have cabin nine instead. "It's my lucky number is all."

"Yeah, and all that luggage I don't see says to me this is *his* lucky day," the woman cackled lustily. "Nine ain't for rent. Two's what you got. Take it or leave it."

"I'll take it." J.D. took the key, winking at the old biddy, turning on the charm. "Are you sure you aren't related to Hepburn?"

Ann shook her head at him as he opened the door to two. "You are shameless."

"You just need a little imagination, Ann. Then you'd see the resemblance. I'm sure of it." She sat down on the bed, still huddling inside her coat. J.D. stripped off his jacket, flannel and undershirt, then went straight to the bathroom and stuck his head under the cold shower, long before it had time to warm up. He came out with a towel around his head, gooseflesh all over his chest and shoulders. The healing wound under his arm still looked awful. "You going to pick the lock on nine, or shall I?"

"I thought I'd knock first." She couldn't not notice his muscled torso or the chill of his flesh or its effect on his chest hair and nipples. Couldn't not notice that it was her own breathing she wasn't managing well. "How do you stand that?"

"I'm tough. You're a pansy. Go ahead and knock. Get it out of your system."

She gave him a look she hoped was stern and not mesmerized as she took a couple of hat pins out of a small silk clutch in her purse. "You need to go soak your head some more. Your disposition is unacceptable."

He wiped his face once more with the ridiculously inadequate bath towel and let his hand stray down his chest with the cloth. Her failure to say to him that nothing was going to happen between them loomed as over-large as his shoulders in the dumpy little crackerbox of a motel room.

"I don't think it's my disposition that's got you all fuddled. Are you hungry, Annie Tschetter, or is it only your eyes?"

Her chin went up. She only knew how to be defiant because indifference to him wasn't anywhere to be found in her arsenal. "You need to stop calling me that."

"Annie Thorne," he accommodated, tossing the towel aside, baring his chest.

She should have thrown away those button-down jeans. "Ann. Just...Ann. Calder if you prefer."

She needed not to sit there like a doe trapped by the eyes and intent of a stag. There was a fifteen-year-old boy out there falsely accused of a heinous crime, on the run for his life, for no reason than that he had been born to her.

"You get dressed. I'll go find out if Mr. Burgess is here or not."

He nodded. He knew as well as she that they had no time to squander.

She walked out the door, closing it quietly behind her, dragging in the bitingly cold, fresh air she'd been only too glad to get out of a few minutes before. The temperature had not gotten above five below zero though the sun shone brightly. With the wind-chill, she thought, subtract another ten or fifteen degrees. If Jaz was out in this, he was in trouble.

She hurried down the sidewalk to cabin nine and rapped on the door. "Mr. Burgess? Roy? Are you in there?" She knocked and called out again when she got no answer. She twisted the doorknob, which was locked, but it got her a response.

"Get the gol-durned hell outta here. I'm not answering one more stupid question." His voice sounded slurred to her, as if he'd been drinking.

She began to argue with him to distract his attention as she went to work with her hat pins. She had just tripped the tumblers when Thorne appeared at her side. She stuck the pins in her mouth and opened the door. It gave only four or so inches with the inside chain in place.

Burgess began bellowing as J.D. gave the door one sharp shove, breaking the chain off the door. They ducked quickly inside. The portly old man was trying to get up off the bed and only managed to drop his fifth of vodka.

Ann closed the door.

J.D. snatched up the bottle before most of the liquor spilled. It was hard to tell how much he'd drunk. "Roy, settle it down. No call to getting your shorts in a knot." He gave an assist as the old guy struggled to sit up. He seemed to Ann more physically infirm than drunk. "We're not the cops," J.D. assured him. "We're not the press. We're here because we believe what you said about Jaz not being responsible for that fire, Roy, and we need your help."

"Yeah, you'n every other durned Tom, Dick and Harry."

Sitting now on the foot of the rickety bed, Ann exchanged looks with J.D. and shivered violently. Though he could mean the press, chances were at least equal that one of the TruthSayers had gotten to Burgess ahead of them.

She had to wonder if there was any real possibility of sorting it out with him.

"I'm done doin' any talking," he growled. His hand shook like mad as he lifted the bottle of vodka to his lips.

J.D. took gentle but firm hold of the rickety wrist. They had a duel of clashing glances. "If you care for that boy, Roy, you'll help us out here."

"Ah, hell's bells. That boy and me go back before he was even born, so don't be thinkin' I don't care about the little bugger."

Still crouched at the side of the bed, Thorne looked at her again, the question in his eyes. She nodded. In an awful sort of parody, old Roy began nodding off sitting up on the side of the bed. J.D. gave him a shake. "Roy, this woman sitting here with us? Do you remember her?"

He looked toward her as if he hadn't realized at all that she was still there, then as if he could no more distinguish her from any other woman than he could fly. "Why should I?"

"Because, Mr. Burgess," she offered and pulled off the ski cap, letting her red hair spill wildly out about her shoulders. "Jaz was my baby."

"Holy cow!" Tears flooded up in his rheumy brown eyes and spilled out into his snowy whiskers. "Annie? Pregnant little Annie?"

"It's me, Mr. Burgess. Yes. Remember, John and Edith were at a church meeting when I had to go to the hospital? You drove me. You even waited around until Jaz was born—"

"To see if we would get a little girl or a little boy." His hand shook all the way to the nightstand where he put down the bottle. "You should have never left that boy, Annie. God rest those gentle people, but Jaz never fit with Zimmer, and that Edith, she didn't know how to say no or control the boy." More tears welled up in his eyes. "Why did you go?"

Tears glazed her own eyes so much, old Burgess was little more than a watery blur. "I didn't...I should never have done that."

J.D. shot her a look. They had no time for her self-recriminations either. "Roy, you've got to listen up now. Tell us who else came around that seemed to be looking for Jaz."

"They were all lookin' for the boy." The old guy seemed to straighten up a little. "Cops 'n all. They think he firebombed his house. The boy needs some serious straightening around, but he didn't do that. I'd stake everything on it, and that's the tooth...uh, truth." He swayed a bit, then heaved himself up off the bed. "I gotta go to the can."

J.D. stayed with him till he got into the bathroom in case he fell, then turned around and switched on the ten-inch black-and-white television sitting on the battered dresser. The noon news was on all the channels. Jaz was the big story on every affiliate.

J.D. quickly homed in on the station with the clearest reception, in time to catch a glimpse of the half burned-out house with the gently winding sidewalk Ann had walked hundreds of times.

He stood staring at replays of the blaze, taken from both ground level and news helicopters. Then, to the accompaniment of old Roy Burgess throwing his guts up, Ann saw a ninth-grade school photo of Jason Adam Zimmer. Her baby, grown to his precarious teen years, accused now of not only the arson but the murder of his adoptive parents.

Jason.

Her fingers flew to her lips to control the trembling.

His hair, she thought, was like hers in black-and-white photos, and his eyes. There was an attitude about Jaz in that photo that worried her, but he had fine, still-immature features that would make him into a handsome young man in a few more years.

If he lived a few more years.

The things they were saying about him made her want to throw something.

"It's the news, Ann. Don't let it get under your skin." J.D. turned down the volume, sat on the end of the bed to learn what else was being reported and pulled her beside him.

The television news anchor cut to a single line from an interview with Roy Burgess. The grocer was shown agreeing that the boy had been in juvenile court on numerous occasions. Roy had obviously been edited. Then the reporter still on the scene resumed. "At this hour, the police have little more to go on than they had in the first few hours after the firebombing occurred late yesterday afternoon. Arson investigators believe the boy may not have intended to cause this much damage to his parents' home."

"Or maybe," Ann snapped at the presumption of guilt, "the boy didn't do it at all."

J.D. murmured his agreement with her outrage. "Especially since, even from their point of view, it could also be the work of a pro making the thing look amateurish."

The reporter concluded. "It's been suggested by sources close to the investigation that Jason Zimmer might be making a run for the Canadian border."

"Wonder where that idea came from?" J.D. leaned forward and switched off the set in disgust. He'd lobbed that excuse at the cop who'd answered Ann's call; now it was being reported as if it had any basis in truth.

Ann felt chilled to the bone. The TruthSayers were

playing everything very close to the vest. She had to wonder for what occasion or purpose they were holding back from the press the fact that Jaz was her natural son. Hard to imagine in what way they might later exploit that tidbit.

"Do you think Jaz might have run north?"

J.D. scowled at the door to the bathroom, a scant three feet away, and stood. "Burgess is the only one who might know. I'm going to go dunk ol' Roy's head too."

"Thorne, he's old," she protested, "and he was so good to me—"

"Ann, I didn't mean it literally." He looked down at her as if he wished she knew him better than to think he would abuse an elderly man who had not only taken a sixteen-year-old girl to the hospital, but stayed to be sure she and her baby were all right. "I'm not going to hurt him."

She felt like a shrew. "I'm sorry. I know that. It's just—"

"I know. Me too." He put his hands on his narrow hips, shaking his head in frustration. "That fire…" The toilet flushed and the faucet came on in the bathroom. He sat down with her again. "I hate them. I just keep flashing on a fire in this little diner in the town where I grew up. The mother of one of my friends owned the place. She died of burns and smoke inhalation. I can't imagine a worse way to die."

"You're thinking whoever did this knew that about your history? That this—" Her voice failed. She gritted her teeth and went on, her hand on his biceps. "That this attack was tailored to get your attention?"

"It wouldn't surprise me at all." His jaw tightened. "It never fails to amaze me how much these vigilante bastards know."

The water stopped running in the next room and Roy opened the door. He came out, looking hard at Ann, trying, she thought, to reassure himself that he was not dreaming or suffering some alcohol-induced delusions. She had never seen him drink all those years ago, never heard so much as a whisper that he drank too much. Maybe he'd only gotten good and drunk now because he felt so bad for Jaz.

They both had to get up to let Roy pass by in the narrow space between the end of the bed and the dresser. He dropped heavily into the sparse, scarred Danish-modern chair beside the door with its chain lock broken.

J.D. got up and sat instead on the side of the bed facing him. "Roy, do you have any idea where to find Jaz?"

"Some." He looked at Ann again, accusingly. "You should have stayed in touch, little girl."

"I want to help Jaz now, Roy." They couldn't afford much time to appease him. "Anything you tell us, I promise you, we'll use to help him."

J.D. tried to reassure the old man as well. "We have some idea who was responsible for the fire, and for making it look as if Jaz had done it. These are very dangerous people, Roy. If there's any possibility one of them went after Jaz, we don't have a minute to lose."

Burgess sucked on his teeth for a couple of seconds, considering, she thought, that he had no other way of helping Jaz himself. "The boy took a car off

my property. Side of the grocery beside the alley.
You remember that T-Bird I had?''

"The one you drove to the hospital when I went
into labor?'' She nodded. ''I think so. It was yellow,
wasn't it?''

"That's the one. Been sitting back of the grocery
five years. Haven't done a thing to keep the old thing
running, but Jaz has had his eye on it for a couple
years. Must have fixed it up between sacking and
stocking. He's a regular whiz at mechanical things.''

"Is it still yellow, Mr. Burgess?'' She didn't know
why she still used mister, except that it came so naturally to her tongue. When he nodded she asked
again if he knew where Jaz would go. ''North, do
you think, to the border?''

Roy scoffed. ''The boy's got no idea about things
like that. Why would he?''

"Television, maybe,'' J.D. offered.

"Nope. He's got no use for that kinda drivel.
Tombstone. That's what he likes. *Butch Cassidy*.
Westerns, you know. *Dances with Wolves*. Things
like that. You want my idea, he'd take himself off to
the Outlaw Canyon down south in the Bighorn
Mountains. Hole in the Wall country near to Kaycee.''

"Wyoming, then?'' J.D. asked.

"Be my guess.''

"Mr. Burgess, that's a huge help.'' The information was really more than either one of them had
dared hope for, despite what a massive amount of
territory there was to the infamous Hole in the Wall
country. ''Did you tell anyone else any of this?''

"One guy. Told me he was a teacher of Jaz's up
at the junior high. Said he's real sorry about all this

trouble coming down on the boy now.'' Looking back on that conversation, Burgess seemed to get agitated. ''Now to think, he kinda tricked me.''

J.D. asked how.

''Said, where'd a kid like Jaz go? Cops think he did it, says this guy, sure as shootin' they aren't gonna cut Jaz any slack. He's got to get clean outta the territory, he says, or they'll fry him. Kinda like Butch Cassidy 'n the Sundance Kid.''

''All this from the guy who said he was a teacher, Mr. Burgess?''

''Yeah, him,'' Burgess confirmed. His eyes watered. The tiny broken veins on his bulby old nose seemed to grow a brighter red.

''So,'' J.D. phrased carefully, ''was it you or this teacher who first mentioned the Hole in the Wall?''

''It was me, for positive sure. But it's kind of uncanny the way he brought up Butch Cassidy.''

''Did this teacher have any other bright ideas?''

''Some plain duds, more. Like, maybe Jaz'd try hoppin' a train to California. Or...let's see.'' Burgess seemed to focus somewhere inside his head. ''Asked if I took him in or if he had any friends that'd get a charge outta helping Jaz hide out. That sort.''

Ann exchanged brief glances with J.D. The old man had been grilled by a pro. There was really nothing uncanny or coincidental in bringing up Butch Cassidy and the Hole in the Wall Gang, just a clever, chatty, unthreatening elimination of possibilities until he struck pay dirt. It probably hadn't taken the teacher much longer than it had taken Burgess to volunteer the information now.

''So, do you believe he really was one of Jaz's teachers?''

"I didn't call the junior high school, but I can tell you when he left he got back into a pickup truck with California plates." His eyes teared up yet again, obviously fearful that he had said the wrong thing to the wrong person. "I didn't get the number. Didn't think of it. Never thought there'd be a reason, you know?"

J.D. nodded respectfully. "What color was the pickup?"

"Brown, I think. Looked fairly new. Sorta bronze."

"And was there some reason you did notice the plates, Mr. Burgess?"

"Well, this teacher was snooping around the corner before he drove off. I saw him sort of looking around by the alley. He'd have probably seen where the old car was parked because there'd be no snow there, and there'd be tracks. Then he went across the street to the neighbors. I didn't tell him about the T-Bird, but if he asked, they mighta told him what car was there."

J.D. nodded; Ann felt sick, alternately fevered with rage and chilled with fear for her innocent son. The whole point of the firebombing of the Zimmers' home had been to flush them out of the Cold Springs colony, but the TruthSayers would not have neglected to put someone into a position to nab Jaz should he run. If all else failed, they could count on J. D. Thorne giving himself up in exchange for Jaz.

J.D. looked at Mr. Burgess. "Roy, I have a problem with your staying on here."

"I'm not going home. Those TV people won't find me here."

"I'm afraid they might. If we found you, others

won't be far behind. Would you be willing to let me put you up in a nice hotel in Billings for a week or so?''

"Don't see the use of it, really.''

"We just want you to be safe, Mr. Burgess,'' Ann urged the old man. "Away from anyone else who might want to know what you've told us bad enough to hurt you.''

BY THE TIME they had each taken a brief shower at the motel on the highway to Clyde Park, then driven as far as Billings, the sun had begun to set. They deposited Roy Burgess in a suite on the concierge floor of one of the better hotels belonging to a national chain, and paid in advance fifteen hundred dollars for ten days on the "Altman'' credit card that would alert Matt and Garrett.

They'd chosen the hotel from the Billings phone book for its proximity to an army surplus store from which they outfitted themselves with minimal winter hiking and camping equipment. They chose binoculars, a battery-operated lantern and a couple of new mummy bags good for temperatures to fifty below zero, then jeans, sweaters and several pairs of long underwear, men's for J.D., boy's for her. All of it fit into a large backpack with J.D.'s packing expertise.

On the outskirts of the city, they stopped for gas, bought a half-dozen burritos and a map of Wyoming. Ann unwrapped burritos and checked the map as J.D. headed east on I–90. The roads were dry; the winter, they'd been told, had been mild in the Bighorns, so the weather seemed not to be an issue, but J.D. thought the Hole in the Wall canyon must parallel the southern end of the Bighorn Mountains for fifty miles or more.

After an extended study of the map by the light of a small flashlight, Ann confirmed J.D.'s fears. Finding Jaz in that country would be more difficult than the proverbial needle in the haystack—if he were alone. And if he had the skills to survive in wilderness areas by himself.

But if the guy in the brown pickup truck, the teacher whom they had to assume was in fact one of the TruthSayers, had caught up with Jaz, the teacher now held all the cards, and Jaz had become the bait in the trap set for J.D. In that scenario, there would be a trail of clues left to lure him to his death in the attempt to free Jaz.

In the mountains, even in a mild Wyoming winter, the possibilities for killing J.D. without detection were almost endless.

They would have to kill Ann as well, but even when they both disappeared, there would be no one screaming foul. They could be painted as ignorant, inexperienced greenhorns who'd gone into the mountains without the necessary precautions or supplies.

J.D. had no intention of letting that happen, but with Jaz in the hands of the enemy, any prediction was worse than useless.

Five miles south of Hardin, Montana, he asked about alternate roads into Wyoming besides I-90. "I don't know which is worse, crossing the state line on the interstate, or on a secondary highway."

Ann turned on the small flashlight again and studied their choices. "There's only one alternative. A county road, it looks like, that follows a river for a while before it crosses the line into Wyoming. If you want it, we can get off I–90 at Lodge Grass. That's coming up pretty soon. What are you thinking?''

"The interstate is a more likely spot for a road-block."

She had been so consumed with worry for Jaz, she'd lost track for a while of the danger to J.D. Someone wanted him dead, and wanted it so much that the ruthless firebombing of innocent victims was nothing more than a ruse cruelly, cleverly designed to snag J.D.'s attention.

"Would they really do that? Stop every car on every interstate looking for us?"

"They've got no choice, Ann. They don't know where we are or what we're driving."

"How can you be sure of that?" But his skeptical look gave it away. If he'd been seen, he'd have been ambushed before now, long since dead. "All right, but the same logic goes for an alternate route. I can't imagine a better place for an ambush than a deserted secondary road."

"Neither can I." He gave her a conspiratorial sort of grin meant to make light of a deadly set of alternatives. "Wanna be my gun moll?"

She played along and pretended to think over his offer. "What would that make you?"

"A desperado, of course."

"You look the part," she teased. He thought the desperado image went a ways down the road to pleasing her. "Are you ever going to shave again?"

"No." He flashed on the moment in Manny's chop shop when he'd seen himself as Samson to her Delilah. He'd play any role opposite her. Clyde to her Bonnie.

"That's fairly firm."

"I had to fit in in Cold Springs, didn't I?"

"We're not in Kansas anymore, Toto."

Another image knocked loose in his mind, of himself sitting in Martin Rand's living room, Rand saying the prosecution team in Vorees's trial intended to lose the case. He'd thought then that he hadn't heard Rand right, *or else he wasn't in Kansas anymore.*

"What is it, J.D.?"

"I just flashed on the afternoon with Rand."

"*The* afternoon?"

He nodded and explained how Kansas had triggered the memory. The white lines marking the divided lanes on the interstate seemed almost to meld into one solid line as the recollection took a more definite shape as well. "I watched your testimony on a closed-circuit right after lunch."

Watched her, thought of her. Wanted her. Remembered one more time the impact on his soul of that first kiss.

He took his eyes off the melding white line on the highway and looked at her in the dim green glow of the dash lights. "I wasn't in a good mood, Ann. I was wondering what in the hell had possessed me to promise you that I wouldn't come around when we got back to Seattle."

Against the dash lights, he watched the silhouette of her face, saw the delicate shape of her throat go up and then down.

"I—"

"You don't have to say anything." He wished he hadn't started that, because it had nowhere to go on I–90 in a Jeep for which he didn't have a license, on the way to rescue a hell-bent but innocent teenager who was a son she'd never known. "Just so you know. Even before I got to Rand, I was thinking about you. About us."

Her head dipped. "What else did Rand say?"

He cleared his throat and focused again on his driving and the mesmerizing white line. "I don't...he was making some argument—" He broke off and swore softly. "He reminded me of the section of the state statutes that gives the district attorney the discretion not to prosecute." He cited the reference. "Even with ample evidence, if he thinks bringing the case to court will—quote, unquote—'diminish respect for the law.'"

Her jaw slackened in disbelief. "Are you saying that all the work you've done to root out the dirty TruthSayer cops is going to be buried in the *interests* of law enforcement?"

He nodded, clearly recalling the urge to smash something with his empty bottle of beer. "I remember thinking that Rand had probably handed the D.A. the strategy on a silver platter himself."

Ann rubbed her temple. "J.D., is Rand one of them? Is that what you're saying?"

Maybe he'd only thought he knew the feeling of betrayal. "It would sure explain a lot of things, wouldn't it? Why I showed up at your place. Why there happened to be people listening to Samuel spilling his guts."

She looked stricken to him, as if she'd been taken unaware where it made more sense to have been on high alert. "Does it explain the shooting?"

"Oh, God," he uttered, knocked off his pins by the absolute, brutal clarity of her reasoning.

Rand.

Chapter Eleven

He clamped his mouth shut and gripped the wheel to expend the raw, raging energy of his emotions. Looked at dispassionately, without the blinders of friendship and unquestioned loyalty, the *years,* the sheer weight of their history together, Rand made exquisite sense as the force behind the attempt on J.D.'s life.

Looked at from Rand's power-mongering mind-set, bringing his oldest friend to Seattle, getting him on the TruthSayers undercover task force was a stroke of corrupt genius. Their history together played in Rand's favor.

Somehow, whether it was in the legal strategy or in some way J.D. hadn't yet fathomed, it was Rand's chimes he had rung, Rand who was threatened by J.D.'s refusal to back off the investigation into TruthSayers penetration of legitimate law enforcement.

His fingers shaped fists around the steering wheel. He could think of nothing to say, nothing to redeem himself overlooking time and again what his instincts had told him. "Blind, *stupid* loyalty." Out of his mouth, the word sounded vile.

"J.D., we don't *know* anything. There are other explanations—"

"Yeah, like what?"

"Maybe someone else caught up with you that night. Someone who thought if you were dead, your investigation would just dry up and blow away. You really can't rule out any of the cops or attorneys who've been suspended pending Warren Remster's review." If the D.A. failed to bring charges, the suspensions would be lifted and the officers, attorneys and staff members compensated.

She drew his attention to the signs directing them off I–90 to the county road.

He left it up to her. "You want to stick with the interstate?"

"Might as well."

He nodded and drove on.

"The other thing," she pointed out, "is that even if Rand did give Remster the idea, would Rand really be so threatened by your knowing what he'd done that he'd try to have you murdered? I haven't gotten the impression from you that he could be so insecure—"

"He's not."

"Then maybe Rand called the marshal service with only the intention of helping you—"

"Saving me from myself? You're a good one to argue that, Ann."

She looked at him as if he'd hit her.

He felt like a first-class heel, throwing that back in her face. "I'm sorry. That was uncalled for."

She waved off his apology. "You're right, Thorne. I don't even know Martin Rand. But it is possible that Remster came up with the strategy himself to avoid protracted hassles with the police brass. As for Samuel, it's also possible there were TruthSayers sympathizers sitting in the bar anyway.''

He reached over and took her hand, threaded his blunt fingers through her much smaller ones, forcing himself to back off attacking her for defending the possibility that Martin Rand wasn't a traitor.

His jaw ached with tension, and for the first time in hours, maybe a day, he felt the throbbing in his head again. Flames licked at the edges of his mind, the images on the black-and-white television in Clyde Park, images older than that. Much older. ''All I'm saying, Ann, is that it wouldn't be the first time I let loyalty interfere with my better judgment.''

''I don't think you were letting it interfere! That's my point. Did you call Rand on it? Did you ask him if he told Remster how he could get out of those prosecutions?''

He knew he wouldn't have let it go. He'd never pulled punches with Rand, but he couldn't recall taking him on.

She closed her fingers around his. ''You're beginning to remember things. More than yesterday,'' she added, a hopeful note in her tone.

He fell silent as they crossed the border into Wyoming. He just didn't know how to disabuse her of her hope. Her point concerning Rand's lack of any insecurities didn't contradict the case to be made against Rand, but reinforced it.

Rand knew what he was doing. Always had. It took that kind of belief in his own decisions to be a magistrate on the federal bench.

The miles passed. I–90 crossed over the Tongue River, swung east of Sheridan, then headed southeasterly. Ann sat quiet and still too long. J.D. didn't mind a silence between them, but this was of a pensive quality that reminded him of their last trip into Wyoming when it was Kirsten and Garrett's son Christo whose life hung in the balance.

"You want to talk about it?"

"I was just thinking—" She cleared her throat, faked a hand through her hair to obliterate a tear with the inside of her wrist. "Maybe this is one of those times when you're letting loyalty overtake your better judgment."

He doubted very much that he wanted to hear this. "Spit it out."

"All right." The steely resolve he had seen before in her, admired in her, might as well have been a banner she ran up her flagpole. "You don't have to do this. You shouldn't be doing this."

He glanced at her overlong. He knew for certain now that he didn't want to hear this. "Don't have to do what, Ann?"

"Go after Jaz."

His jaw took on that implacable cast. "That's what I thought you meant."

"I'm serious, J.D."

"I'm not laughing."

"You're not listening—"

"Don't." His voice warned her, *not another syllable.*

She would not be stifled. Her flag waved on. "J.D., you're playing right into their hands out of some misguided loyalty or sense of obligation to me—"

"Is that what you think this is?"

"J.D., yes! It's who you are, it's what you do! It's

why I fell so hard—'' She broke off, pressing her small fist to her lips, refusing to look anywhere but into the pitch-black of night.

''What? In love with me?'' He wanted to slam on the breaks, drag her from the Jeep and wait on the side of he road in the bitter cold until she said the words.

He thought hell might freeze over first.

He refused to lose the time it would take. Maybe he should have anyway. The bitterness spilling out of his mouth betrayed everything he felt for her. ''Which part, Ann? The loyal part or the misguided part? Because you know, I'm clearly unable to separate the two, so maybe—''

''J.D., don't! You know what I mean. Maybe you are loyal to a fault. Maybe I am in love with you. No,'' she uttered, low from somewhere deep inside her, ''let's be absolutely clear. I *am* in love with you. I am in love with everything about you! But playing into their hands, playing their game at all *is* insane. Suppose you don't go after him. Suppose I—''

''Suppose you what, Ann?'' His teeth clamped shut but he couldn't keep his mouth shut or the sarcasm out of his words. She had said to him what an hour before he would have sold his soul to hear, so only now did he understand exactly of what mettle she was made to say she was in love with him, with everything about him, in order to have her own way in getting between him and his insanely misguided decisions. ''Go ahead. This should be good! If you ask them, 'Pretty please, sirs, may I have my son back?' Is that what you're thinking?''

''That's not—''

''Period, end of sentence, what it's *not* is up for a

damn vote,'' he yelled at her. ''Chalk sincerity right up there with misguided loyalty, Ann, because I'm not changing my mind. I stood by and watched in Cold Springs while your friends and family held out against the bastards, and it isn't going to happen like that again. Not on my watch. *I'm* the one they want. It's your *son* they've got. What do you think will happen if I ignore them?''

An awkward little sound, nothing resembling words, came out of her in answer. He warned himself that he could be no less brutal with the truth than she was, no matter that his heart cleaved to believe he would have to die to restore her son to her. ''If you think they won't kill him, Ann, think again. If it hasn't been made fairly clear to you what the bastards are capable of, I don't know what it will take.''

She fell silent again down the lonely stretch of highway south of Sheridan. No doubt he had been brutal enough, or that she understood his intent. He had passed Piney Creek, then Exit 51 to Lake de Smet when he topped a hill and came in sight of the taillights of another southbound car.

A Lexus sedan, top of the line. The car seemed to speed up for a half mile or so, then slowed dramatically.

Alert in spite of it all, Ann straightened. Her hand went automatically to her weapon, holstered beneath her left arm. ''What is he doing?''

J.D. swore. ''He's either drunk or we're in deep trouble.'' He signaled to pass the luxury sedan, which increased its speed again and moved left as well. J.D. shoved harder on the gas, then backed off when he saw the glint of chrome on the back of spotlights mounted near the driver's window.

The car was an unmarked cop, slowing now. J.D. fell back into place behind the Lexus despite having to brake to under fifty miles an hour to do it.

He had no other choice save a suicidal break for it.

Two SUVs bearing down fast from behind were cops as well, their lights coming on at once, flashing ominously out of sync, like flames in a night sky.

Tersely he ordered Ann to drop her seat back down.

The Jeep was unequipped to do that. She slammed the entire seat back as far as it would go, pulled her weapon and slid to the floor as J.D. jerked the steering wheel hard to the far side of the southbound interstate then the other, careening within a breath of rolling the Jeep.

He expected at any moment rounds of ammo fired indiscriminately, intended to explode his gas tank and torch the Jeep. When that didn't happen, he judged that they might try to take him down alone.

He wouldn't go easily and he especially would not go down in a way that took Ann with him or failed to expose the night's work for a bloody, ruthless ambush.

"Hold on!" His heart thudding, his mind racing, his instincts firing on all cylinders, he gauged to the split second the instant in which to slam on the brakes. The back end of the vehicle veered off the pavement, hurtling across the barrow pit alongside the highway. The Jeep bounced to a dead stop at a ninety-degree angle with the roadway, leaving beneath it room to maneuver.

To one side, two men got out and went into firing stances behind the sedan; to the left, another, behind him still another. Pulling his own weapon from his shoulder holster, J.D. jerked open the handle, threw his shoulder into the door and fell through the narrow wedge to the ground.

He stretched his body long and rolled under the Jeep, then fired from his belly at the tires of the sedan to the right and the SUVs to the left, blowing in five rounds of ammunition the right front and rear tires on the two nearest vehicles, and the front tire of the last.

Then the desperate shouts into a bullhorn. "Thorne, for the love of God, hold your fire!"

Above him the heat off the engine, below the frozen naked earth, around him the scent of hot motor oil and scorched rubber consumed the air. He didn't know what he heard, what he expected. Adrenaline roared through him as if a dam had burst. Though he trusted her to take care of herself, he could only think of Ann, still vulnerable in the Jeep if the thing went up in flames, but there was no gunfire returned, no explosions, no threats, no action to take.

"Thorne?" came the shout through the bullhorn. "Rosebud? You hear me?"

The nickname, roughly akin in eighties Telluride teenage lingo to 'pantywaist,' came at him as if through a warp in time. "Everly? Kyle?"

"No. Hanifen. Johnson County sheriff, Dex Hanifen. Everly sent me to give you protection. Escort you in. What say you put down your weapon so we can we talk like civilized men?"

J.D. NEGOTIATED THEIR surrender until Hanifen agreed to ride with them in the still-functional county four-wheel drive, unarmed, under Ann's guard. All five of the other men were left stranded on the highway with their weapons and keys locked in the trunk of the disabled Lexus.

It was no more than ten or twelve miles outside of Buffalo, Wyoming, up Highway 116, to the ranch house of the Bar Naught, owned and operated, Hanifen told them as he gave J.D. directions, by Kyle Everly.

With its impeccable, impractical white fencing, the ranch yard looked more as if it belonged on a fine old Kentucky bluegrass estate than in the frozen foothills of the Bighorn Mountains.

A powerful-looking older man, perhaps fifty, trotted out as J.D. pulled the Explorer to a stop in the graveled circular driveway. The sheriff asked him to see to retrieving the men who'd been left stranded on the highway. Then a man garbed in a long fur coat emerged from the enormous stone house onto a veranda, stepping lightly down the stairs to greet them.

This must be Everly. Ann knew the name before she met the man, nothing more except that he had grown up in the same small Colorado town of Telluride as J.D. The seeming coincidences bothered her a lot. Rand had brought J.D. to Seattle, maybe betrayed him.

Everly hailed from the same town. Same years, same friends, and somehow he managed to be in the right place at the right time with whatever influence and money could buy to supposedly bring J.D. to safety.

Standing now in a stylish, masculine mink coat, his breath puffing into clouds of moisture, Everly gave a striking, half-apologetic grin. "My posse, so to speak."

She had seen unnaturally beautiful men before, known them, knew their vanity. Kyle Everly was of a slight build, a head shorter than J.D., but with stunning features, dark eyes and flawless blond hair.

J.D. was not amused even now, despite Everly's easy charm, by the so-called posse. The word itself bothered her as well, its associations too close to vigilante justice, still more because even on first impression, Everly didn't seem to be unwitting or insensitive.

J.D. wasn't going to let it go either. "Men get killed that way, Kyle."

"Only if you're trigger-happy," he retorted, intending to be disarming. He shot the sheriff a look to confirm, she thought, that none of his men had fired back on J.D. Hanifen nodded in response but he was staying clear of the argument. Everly went on. "You have a bone to pick about it, Thorne," he chided, "why don't you turn around and notice you still have your ass intact?"

J.D. stood toe to toe with him, got in the slighter man's face. "I do have a bone to pick with it, but I suppose if you could understand that, you just wouldn't be you."

"Come on, man. Lighten up. If I didn't know how good you are, how easily you'd have slipped through the fingers of two or three men, I wouldn't have sent six. I'll pick up the tab on the tires, so no one's any the worse for wear. You needed help, you're going to get it. Why don't we go inside and—"

"Thing is, I don't recall asking for help."

"No? Well, that's not what Rand led me to believe."

She wanted to know as badly as J.D. exactly what Martin Rand had told Everly, but she couldn't stand there in the cold anymore. The temperature had to be near zero and she wanted desperately to use the facilities. "Could we go inside to continue this?"

Everly begged her pardon, turning on the wattage. They hadn't yet gotten round to introductions. "Sorry, ma'am. Of course we should go in. What do you say, J.D.?"

In answer he turned on his heel and stalked off toward the house. Everly blinked and held out a genteel arm to her.

She declined, tucking her hands beneath her arms, watching J.D.'s back. "Thanks, but I'm fine. I'm—"

"Detective Ann Calder, I presume. Woman of the hour."

"I don't know about that."

"Never doubt it. Anyway, I'm Kyle Everly." He leaned in toward her as they walked over crunching snow, talking softly, confidentially. "You'll have to cut us some slack. J.D. and I go way back with the butting-heads routine. He's really shell-shocked, yes?"

Climbing the wide veranda stairs, she had the feeling he expected confidences in return. "I think anyone would be, when there are lives at stake and no one left to trust."

"Giving away nothing," he said, smiling.

"No charity." She didn't smile back.

"Anyway." He grimaced, almost prettily. "Maybe I can help. That's all I intended, by the way."

Hanifen stood holding the door ajar. Everly took it over and held the door open for her, ushering her inside a foyer thirty feet high, and as deep. The floor was hardwood, its dark patina gleaming. There were no animal-head trophies mounted on the walls, no extravagant rifle displays, only tasteful western art. A pair of Georgia O'Keeffe paintings, numerous bronzes. Everything in sight was saturated in wealth without seeming ostentatious or overdone.

Everly's housekeeper was hanging J.D.'s coat in a closet behind an elegantly carved pocket door. Everly shed his own, and took Ann's while Hanifen hung his hat.

He pointed out the direction of the powder room, and indicated where the three men would meet in a substantial library to the left of the foyer.

By the time she returned, the housekeeper had only just served hot toddies. Ann accepted one and sat on a deep, upholstered settee beside J.D. From a cursory look around, the library housed as eclectic a collection of books as could be found in any private home in the world.

Everly and Hanifen sat in matching premier-quality oxblood leather wing chairs.

J.D. had waited so she would miss nothing. He sat forward on the settee. "Okay, so what about Rand?"

Everly clipped a cigar, then lighted its tip, puffing gently. Ann had never seen anyone smoking with quite his élan. "Rand called, J.D. A couple of days ago. Friday, I guess it was. He's worried about you." His shapely eyebrows went up. "With cause, you'll admit."

"That depends on what has him worried."

"For starters, the assault on your life. How the hell did you survive that one?"

J.D. shrugged. "Just lucky I guess."

Everly didn't smile. Ann thought he was adapting himself to J.D.'s unreceptive attitude.

"You remember what my old man used to say?" He looked at Ann briefly to explain. "My dad got into every kind of accident you can imagine. Rolled a couple of cars, torched himself along with the grand finale of the fireworks one year. That kind of thing." He hesitated briefly to leave space in the conversation for an answer from J.D., then went on. "People used to tell him how lucky he was to survive those things more or less intact."

He looked at J.D. again and came to his point. "Dad used to say if he was so lucky, those things wouldn't happen in the first place. Point is, Thorne, you may have survived that shootout, but I wouldn't be inclined to say you've been lucky lately."

"Then Rand filled you in on the rest?"

"He did."

"Why don't you start at the beginning, so I have some idea what's going on."

Everly held the cigar easily between his second and third fingers, the ashes hovering by design over a leaded-crystal ashtray. "He didn't say that much at first. Just that you'd been under a lot of pressure with the internal affairs investigations. What do you call it?"

"IIS. Internal Investigation Section," Ann answered softly, fishing for what Everly knew. "But that's the Seattle P.D. You knew J.D. is independent of that?"

"Of course. It was out of Grenallo's office, wasn't it? The assistant U.S. attorney who killed himself?"

J.D. stared at his hands. Trouble brewing there, in his thoughts. She went ahead. "You're very well informed."

Everly gave a slow smile. "For a hick from Wyoming you mean?"

"For anyone not in law enforcement, I meant. Or living outside the Pacific Northwest."

"I'll buy that," Everly conceded. "But since your exploits in and around Jackson Hole early this winter, what with the kidnapping and murders, our coverage of your affairs has been fairly extensive."

She could not have provided a more smooth or compelling explanation, given an hour to think of one. Still, it seemed somehow disingenuous. Too slick. "So, Rand must have called again at some time?"

"Several times." He stubbed out his half-smoked cigar and sat forward much like J.D. "I'll be frank with you, Thorne. I personally thought Rand was getting a little carried away. I mean, you've obviously survived some dicey situations over the years without Rand's intervention. Or mine, for that matter."

"Carried away, how?" J.D. asked.

"In a panicky sense, I'd have to say. He didn't know where you'd gone. The Oregon cops apparently found your car, Ann, last Sunday, abandoned off whatever it is they call the Pacific Coast Highway up there. They discovered the fingerprints of some known felon, which led them to assume you'd actually spirited J.D. off in another direction altogether."

"Then I called him."

"Yes. He has caller I.D., apparently, so he could pinpoint your hideout. He said he tried to send in federal marshals to give you protection, but you refused. He was concerned about your decision making at that point, which is the point at which I thought he was exaggerating.

"I mean, this TruthSayers thing is getting a little overblown if you believe there's one of them hanging around every corner. Or at least, that's what I thought up until that poor Zimmer kid's home was firebombed and his parents were killed." Everly looked at Ann. "I can't tell you how sorry I am, Ann. These fanatics are out of control."

"How do you know there's any connection to me?" she asked, unable to keep the incredulous tone out of her voice.

"That's where Dex, here, comes in. He and I are fairly tight." He looked at the sheriff. "Shoot skeet together. We both belong to a flying club. That sort of thing."

Hanifen nodded. "Everly's mentioned your name in hushed tones of reverence for years now, Thorne." He rolled his eyes. "My friend J.D. this, my friend Rosebud that. Heard you kicked butt on the K.U. football team, about the same time as I was at U.W. getting my clavicles busted for the umpteenth time."

Uninterested in shooting the breeze about college football, J.D. went straight back to the subject. "What about the Zimmers?"

Hanifen's easy manner faded. "I've got a friend who works on the Montana highway patrol. They're keeping a tight lid on the information, so far as the media is concerned. Butts will be busted if the press gets wind of this. The rumors going on around the watering hole have it that the Zimmer kid's biological mother is none other than the female detective who swooped in and saved J. D. Thorne's life against unknown gunmen, etcetera, etcetera.''

Hanifen's smile returned. ''You see your reputations precede you both.''

J.D. didn't like it. Ann felt hot, smothered, unable to breathe. Where had the rumors begun? What did Jaz know about her?

''If that's the rumor,'' J.D. asked pointedly, ''then wouldn't it make sense that firebombing the Zimmer home wasn't the kid's idea?''

''You ask me, *damn* straight,'' Hanifen agreed. ''No way the kid did that. Someone wanting your attention—or maybe Ann's attention—firebombed that house. Is that what you're thinking?''

''Are you saying the cops in Montana know that?'' J.D. demanded.

''Not at all. I'm saying, it'd be obvious to any damn fool but for the facts.''

''What facts?'' Ann asked.

''There's an eyewitness. A neighbor, reputable accountant, no axes to grind, not some near-sighted interfering old biddy. And several of the kid's friends say he's been on the verge of something like this for weeks now.''

''Show me a teenage boy who isn't at that point half the time,'' Everly snapped. ''Hell's bells, Thorne and I blew up an outhouse one time, and if we hadn't gotten caught, that wouldn't have been the end of it, either.''

''You mean, you and Ames,'' J.D. corrected. Ann struggled not to react in some obvious manner to the depth of the ice she heard in his voice. "Maybe Rand."

"Oh, give me a break, Thorne," Everly protested. "If you weren't there that time, there were plenty of other times you were."

"The point we're all making," Hanifen put in, his eyes shifting quickly from Everly to J.D., "is that boy is in trouble. And you're in manure up to your eyeballs, my friend." He met J.D.'s look straight on. He was a large, powerful man though his belly hung over his belt, not one to be intimidated but to do the intimidating. He kept the attitude out of his voice. "If you've got any idea where that kid is, your best bet is to tell me and let us handle it. You know that's the advice you'd be giving any civilian whose kid was in trouble like this."

J.D. ignored the unsolicited advice. "How did you know where to intercept us?"

Hanifen didn't flinch from the barb in J.D.'s question. "We assumed you would come after the boy. He was last seen at the truck stop on I–90. Disappeared into thin air. He'd headed south, you couldn't be far behind."

J.D. straightened. "Someone caught up with Jaz?"

"Way I heard it," Hanifen confirmed. "Can't think how else a fifteen-year-old kid driving a rusted-out old yellow T-Bird is going to escape notice for long. The thing is still at the truck stop and the kid flat disappeared. For all we know, he hitched a ride or hopped inside some semitruck. Anyway, your friend Rand was convinced you'd have figured out where the kid was headed, and since that was apparently south, Everly and I thought a sort of unofficial APB for you was in order. Especially since it sounds like you're the one, J.D., with the price on his head."

Everly lighted his cigar again and sat forward, implying urgency. "J.D., if you've got any idea where the boy is, let Dex handle it. Let me help you." He looked around to encompass all his great wealth. "None of this means anything if I can't help a friend in need."

J.D. blinked. "Thing is, Kyle, I don't know where the Zimmer boy is. And the other thing is, I'm a little tired of help from my friends."

"If you mean Rand—"

"I mean Rand. I mean, you. Tonight. The boy, the Zimmers, the shooting, the warnings. Do I need to go back further than that?"

Everly's teeth clamped down on his cigar. "Rand warned me—"

"I'm sure he did," J.D. cut him off. "What I want to know is if you're as dirty as Rand is, the both of you, or if you're really that gullible."

Everly's angelic features hardened. "I don't think you want to be blowing off your friends, J.D. Not with the kind of enemies you have."

Chapter Twelve

"Funny," J.D. retorted. "I was sort of thinking maybe I'd got my wires crossed back there in that phone booth and confused my friends with my enemies."

Exhausted from their long, sleepless hours, Ann struggled one more time to keep her composure in the face of a terrible pressure to fall apart. If J.D. really believed Everly and his dangerous sidekick sheriff were as dirty as Rand, what in God's name was he thinking, to defy the two of them in their territory and to their faces?

She knew him better than to assume this was recklessness on his part, that he must have his reasons, an agenda for engaging in the verbal shoving match. It was more immediately his own life on the line than Jaz's. Still, she simply couldn't abide another second of their sparring. She stood, interrupting before J.D. had even finished his less-than-subtle accusations.

"Stop it, all of you! This is so pathetic, so beneath you! There is a teenage boy out there somewhere falsely accused of murdering his parents, probably in the hands of lunatics, and all either of you can do is sit there escalating a spitting contest! You make me sick.''

Everly sat back. J.D. would not back off the look, but he toned down his voice. ''If you want to help, we'll need a lift back to the Jeep. We think the boy was headed down to Cheyenne.'' The capital was situated in the southeastern corner of Wyoming along the interstate. ''That's where we were headed—''

''Why Cheyenne?'' Hanifen asked sharply.

J.D. improvised as he went along. ''Apparently, some friend of his moved there a couple of years ago.''

''And you know that because…?''

J.D. looked Hanifen straight in the eye and lied, tossing in the teacher to gauge Everly's reaction as well. ''We talked to one of his teachers from the junior high school.''

Nothing, Ann thought, no reaction from either one of them. Not even the obvious follow-up question to do with how they'd happened across one of the boy's teachers, and an informed one at that.

J.D. grimaced. ''Every minute we sit here jaw-boning the thing, we're losing time.''

Everly quickly agreed. ''I'd be happy to loan you the Explorer. From what I understand, the Jeep you were driving couldn't have been very comfortable. Or if you don't want to wait till my man gets back with that, there's a pickup if you want a four-wheel drive.''

Giving Ann a sympathetic glance, Sheriff Dex Hanifen asked if she believed it would be helpful to alert the authorities along I–25, south through Wyoming and Colorado.

Her chin went up. "Not if Jaz is going to be portrayed as dangerous."

"I'll see to it that he's not, Ann," Everly promised her.

She went to the closet and retrieved their coats from the hovering housekeeper. The tension between the men was thick enough to choke on. Both Everly and Hanifen followed them outside.

As they came down the steps, Everly's bruiser of a groundsman pulled into the heated, ten-car garage in the Explorer. He got out, easily slinging over his shoulder the backpack full of supplies and equipment J.D. and Ann had purchased in the army surplus store.

Everly immediately repeated the offer to J.D. of the Explorer. "Whichever you want, J.D. Take your pick. The garage is on an alarm. The keys are left in the ignition."

J.D. took their backpack off the employee's hands and walked off to put it back into the same vehicle. Ann stuffed her hands deep in her pockets and thanked Everly for the loan in an attempt to apologize for her own outburst and J.D.'s silence. "I'm sorry for the trouble between the two of you."

Everly looked steadily at her. "He's a good man, Ann. I won't take anything away from him, but he needs to think things out a little better." He gave her another perfect smile, however pensive, and joked, "Just don't tell him I told you so."

Not the cold, but something in Everly's too-beautiful features forced the shiver she'd been fighting all night.

"DO YOU THINK either of them believed we're headed to Cheyenne?" Ann asked.

"It's a toss-up. They'll wait and see now."

The question was really one of what they were going to do next. Though no one followed them off Everly's ranch, nor pulled in behind once they hit I–25, there were no towns in the whole of Johnson County in which they could leave Everly's Explorer behind without someone taking notice.

On the other hand, J.D. took as an article of faith that Everly would not have loaned them any vehicle without some way, electronic or otherwise, to track the vehicle's location at all times, which would also have been the case in the Jeep. Either way, the Explorer was in any case, as promised, loaded with luxury options and more than comfortable.

"Do you think I'm overreacting? Paranoid?"

"To think they're somehow involved in this whole thing?" Ann asked only to clarify what he meant. When he nodded, she shook her head. "I never think you're being paranoid, J.D."

He seemed surprised, pleased by her vote of utter confidence. He reached over and took her hand, guiding it back to rest upside down on his thigh. His fingers laced through hers, his thumb lightly stroked her palm.

G-rated as it was, it reminded her of her liberties with his body and the look in his eyes when he'd lain in bed in the bookbinder's hut and watched her taking down her braids.

She felt herself flushing, heating up, breathing differently, needy as a doe in heat for what she hadn't done with a man in sixteen years. Never, for that matter, with a man she loved and honored and respected.

She cleared her throat, made up something to ask him that would bring her back to earth. "What makes you so certain Everly is involved?"

"Because they're scrambling, Ann. Everly and Hanifen both." He shifted in the bucket seat, then sat steering with only one hand along the bottom of the wheel. "I think they've lost track of Jaz and they're nervous."

Too afraid for her teenage son to put any faith in that possibility, she shrugged. "I don't get it."

"They wouldn't have had to go through this little charade if they knew where Jaz had gone."

"Why go through the charade in any case, then? If the whole point of firebombing the Zimmers was to force you out where they could get at you, why didn't they just do it there on the highway? They could have killed us both, J.D., and no one would ever have been the wiser. Mission accomplished. They had to have had enough firepower to outlast us both back there."

Peering into the darkness beyond the headlights, he warned, "They still could. I don't know what their game is, Ann, but if Jaz got away from them, they've got to be worried that someone is onto them. Watching them."

"Do you think Jaz just did get away on his own? Or that someone is helping him?"

"I don't know." He glanced every few seconds into the rearview mirrors as he drove. "A fifteen-year-old kid is pretty resourceful. If I were him, and I had any idea they'd followed me, I'd have jumped into the back of the first truck that came along.

"What worries me," he went on, "is the possibility that he is now as dangerous to the TruthSayers as I am. If he saw who firebombed his house, or saw someone running from there, or if they did catch up with him, and he somehow managed to get away again. In any of those cases, he's a potential eyewitness whether we're talking the arson and murder of the Zimmers or his own kidnapping."

Ann nodded, mute. Her throat felt paralyzed with fear for Jaz. After a moment she found she could talk after all. "That's probably it, isn't it? They now need all three of us dead, so we've got a reprieve until we track him down for them."

He reached across the gearshift console with her hand and rested both their hands on her thigh. "We just have to lose them ourselves. Then, maybe, all three of us will have a chance."

She drew and expelled a long, shaky breath. "Do you have a plan?"

"I'm thinking we repeat what you did with your Honda. Maybe this time hire a wrecker to take the Explorer on down to Cheyenne."

"You're gambling then, that they aren't going to be using spotters along I–25?"

"It's not much of a gamble. Too much room for error in sending people out to watch for us driving by. How much out of our way is it to stay on the interstate till we hit Casper?"

The map she'd bought was back in the Jeep. She checked the glove compartment and found another. Casper was roughly halfway between the north and south borders of the state, too far south by sixty or seventy miles. But Casper was at least a sizable enough city to lose themselves in, and it would only take an hour to drive back north to Kaycee, the blink-of-an-eye town just east of the Hole in the Wall country.

Just as she finished telling him all of that, they came upon Kaycee itself, little more than a widening in the road. Agreeing with her, J.D. stayed on the highway and passed the exit to the state highways leading west into the mountains, 190 and 191. If there was anyone looking out for them, or if there was some kind of tracking device attached to the Explorer, passing Kaycee was a good idea.

And there was nothing they could do in the mountains to begin the search for Jaz until first light.

By MIDNIGHT they arrived in Casper and found an ATM to withdraw a couple thousand dollars, and a twenty-four-hour towing service. J.D. disabled the Explorer and told the tow-truck driver that the vehicle was to be taken down to the Ford dealer in Cheyenne for some obscure parts and repair.

For eight hundred in cash the guy would have transported the vehicle to Albuquerque. For another thousand, he came up with a ten-year-old pickup they could have for a couple of days. J.D. handed over the cash, added five hundred for extra goodwill, and transferred the backpack from the Explorer to the truck.

If there was any tracking device on the Explorer, it would look as if they had gone to Cheyenne. But J.D. made a thorough search of the backpack as well, for any electronic beacon that might have been planted by Everly's man in their possessions, then they headed back north. An hour later, he pulled off the highway in a place concealed by a stand of cedar and cottonwoods along what must have been the bank of the South Fork of the Powder River just south of Kaycee. They unpacked and opened the bedrolls into the back of the truck and slept, spoon-fashion, until dawn.

Stiff and cold, they drove into the town for a hot breakfast. Ann had only just finished, a few minutes after J.D., when she looked out the window beside the booth and shivered violently. J.D. wrenched around to see what had seized her attention, but from his angle in the booth, he couldn't have seen the truck.

"What is it?"

"The teacher's truck. Parked on the northeast corner of the intersection. Bronze, with California plates."

"Let's go." He slid out of the booth, stripped a twenty from his money clip and headed out, leading the way. The truck was parked on the street by a gas station with a couple of service bays already open. J.D. walked up to the nearest open garage door and called out. Ann came up behind him as an old coot in overalls ambled out, wiping his oil-blackened hands on a rag nearly as dirty.

"Can I help ya?"

"I'd be grateful," J.D. answered. "Can you tell me who belongs to that California pickup parked out on the street?"

"Ain't none of my concern," he began, but then stiffened when he saw Ann.

J.D. tensed. "Do you know this woman?"

The grizzled old man shook his head. "No, sirree, I do not. I ain't ever seen her before. But if you've come lookin' for a kid, guy in the pickup with him said to tell any redhead happened by, she's on the right track to hike on up Outlaw Cave way.''

Ann grabbed hold of J.D.'s coat sleeve to steady herself. She had only just been thinking over her oatmeal how terribly remote their chances were of finding Jaz, thinking maybe they shouldn't even be looking at all since the only thing to be accomplished was to bring the three of them conveniently together for the TruthSayers to dispense with. Now, by hook or crook, ill-fated or well, they had their first real piece of information.

"Did you see him?" she asked. "The boy?"

"Not up close—"

"Was he all right?"

"Well, that kinda depends on your point of view. Seemed healthy, if that's what you mean, but I wouldn't a said he was a happy camper.''

J.D. put his arm around Ann's shoulders and grew serious. "We were supposed to meet up with them. This is the boy's mother. We didn't get up here till this morning. Hadn't even decided whether we'd do the Hole in the Wall or the Outlaw Cave." The story they gave the old man needed to seem benign. To imply that Jaz had been kidnapped, or was a runaway, might goad the old man into calling the local cops into the picture. "They must have decided, and like you said, gone on ahead.''

J.D. hesitated and scratched his head. "How'd they get up the canyon if their truck is still here?''

"'Cuz I rode along and drove it on back here.''

"Well, naturally," J.D. responded easily, as if to ask himself why he hadn't thought of that. "They're expecting to ride back out with us.''

But Ann's anxiety for Jaz and J.D. spiraled. Whoever had her son wanted her and J.D. to follow enough that he might as well have left an arrow with their names on it pointing the way. To have any chance of recovering Jaz, she and J.D. would have to hike straight into what could only be an ambush, in the country renowned for exactly that.

He voiced her question. "We had one other guy possibly going to join up with us. Anyone else been around asking after the boy?"

"Nary a one. Wouldn't a said boo if they had, 'less they was a redhead like this'n here," he said, nodding in Ann's direction. The road map of lines on his old face creased more deeply, and he made some noise that said clearly what he thought of hikers going off with such half-baked arrangements to meet and head into the wilderness.

J.D. reinforced the old man's scorn asking for a decent map of the area.

"Got one a my own I can let you see, but I ain't parting with it. They don't make 'em like they used to."

Next to a business license issued to Ike Hanscomb, the map he referred to was tacked on a wall inside the station with yellowed tape probably decades old. He ran a grimy finger along Highway 190 along the Middle Fork of the Powder River until it branched again. "You just keep following along here. Don't get yourselves turned around and head north up the Red Fork."

They left the pickup they'd gotten in Casper off-road maybe a half mile and began hiking beyond where any roads went and through forested areas out of their way that no four-wheel drive would take them.

Old Hanscomb wouldn't part with a map that had probably cost a quarter in its day, but he'd handed over his favorite toy in some weird male-bonding gesture to J.D. The loan was of a satellite global positioning system about the size of a cell phone that Hanscomb used to program in the precise coordinates of fishing holes on Lake de Smet where he wanted to return.

He had programmed the GPS with the degrees longitude and latitude of the Outlaw Cave. The instrument would report to them on their progress both in trajectory and distance remaining.

The cold and the snowy, rugged terrain made the hike in front of them look brutal. At least the sun shone brightly in a cloudless sky. J.D. had hoped they might even find boot tracks in the snow, but he saw none. They would just have to follow their GPS course and hope for the best, akin to having the aid of a magnet to search for the needle in the haystack.

But when he could see the actual lay of the land, J.D. knew they couldn't take the direct route because they would be completely out in the open, exposed and vulnerable to rifle fire. They would have to go higher, through the trees above the deep crevice meadows, and approach the cave from the back side.

A couple of hours in, he stopped by a massive granite boulder three-quarters buried below the ground. The snow had melted off its exposed surface. He released the hip belt of the backpack and shrugged out of it, then got out a handful of high-energy food bars from an outer pouch.

Ann took off her gloves and ate two of them, lost in thought.

"What is it, Ann?"

"I've just been wondering what that was about

between you and Everly when he started talking about blowing up an outhouse.''

He squinted off into the distance. ''There was a time when 'J.D.' was synonymous with 'juvenile delinquent.' The four of us, me, Everly, Ames and Rand, were in trouble all the time. Things like using peashooters to break windows, stealing the old man's car to go joyriding, pop-bottle rockets. Penny-ante stuff like that.''

He polished off another of the food bars, then went on. ''I'm not saying I was any angel, Ann. Not at all. But I knew where the line was drawn between what would get my butt tanned and what would land me in jail.

''I wasn't there when they blew up the outhouse. I was sanding six hundred square feet of a cedar deck for breaking curfew one time too many.''

''Did blowing up the outhouse land them in jail?''

''Not the first time, when I was there, but the third time? You bet it did.''

''So what were you so intense about when he brought it up?''

''I don't know.'' A frown creased his forehead as he crumpled up the food wrapper. ''Everly and Ames were the firebugs. 'Pyros and proud of it,' Everly used to say. Maybe I *am* paranoid, Ann. But, you know, ever since I saw the video of the firebombing of the Zimmers' home, I've been flashing on memories of Ames's mother's diner burnt to the ground, still smoking three days later. Remember?''

''Yes. You were thinking the TruthSayers knew how to get your attention because of that fire when you were kids.''

''Exactly. What I wasn't thinking, then at least,

was that they knew it because Rand was one of them. Then you connected the dots for me between Rand and the attempt on my life.'' He held up a hand to forestall her argument. ''I know you weren't connecting those dots. You're not even convinced Rand is the bad guy here. But then Everly casually drops into the conversation his old exploits—including me—to justify Jaz's being on the verge of firebombing his parents?'' He shook his head. ''It made my skin crawl.''

She wasn't sure she followed the dots he was now connecting for her. ''It isn't a pretty big leap from blowing up outhouses to torching your own mother's diner?''

''Yeah. For ordinary kids it might be. But Ames would do anything on a dare. There was this weird dynamic among the four of us. Everly was a year younger. He'd jumped a grade in junior high. He wasn't the ringleader at all, but he had this…conceit, I guess is the word, like he knew more than anybody else. He usually did. Ames especially was always trying to impress him.''

She hugged her knees to her body. ''Are you saying you think Everly dared Ames to torch his own mother? Or that Everly is one of the TruthSayers and that he ordered the same fate for the Zimmers to remind you? I don't understand why else he would do that, unless he's one of them.''

''If he is, Ann, he's so insulated from the rank and file of the TruthSayers, that in all our years of undercover ops we never heard a whisper of his name.'' He stood, stretching to work out the kinks, then offered her a hand up.

''I know. But—'' She accepted his hand and stood

as well. "That doesn't necessarily mean Everly didn't give Rand the idea, just like Rand gave the D.A. the strategy he needed to duck prosecuting any more TruthSayers cases."

He wished, standing there in the sun on the bone-dry granite, surrounded by evergreen and beyond that fields of snow, that he couldn't see her as her brother Timothy saw her. As a woman meant to be a wife, a mother to a man's children, a beloved helpmate through life.

Or as he saw her himself when they were just a man and woman together, and not picking apart the brutal strategies of criminal minds. A woman with fingers so long and slender and feminine he both remembered and imagined again touching his body. A woman with hair that the sunlight set afire in which he longed to burn his own hands.

A woman with grace and the grit to refuse to be saved from herself. How could he love even that part of her that he knew would turn away from him when this was all over?

His gaze roamed her face, memorizing every nuance of the light and shadow cast on her skin by the sun. She swallowed, maybe fearful of where his looking at her like that would take them, and bowed her head. Her breath came out raggedly.

He lifted her chin with his forefinger. He imagined she would keep her eyes downcast, that he would have to kiss her without seeing what she felt in her soft gray eyes.

He was wrong.

So wrong.

As he lowered his lips to hers, her eyes wide open and exquisitely aware and wanting him, a jolt of fierce, pure, sexual pleasure shot through his body, stiffening his sex, curling his toes, swamping his heart, dimming his wits to anything but her.

He opened his mouth in the kiss and she opened hers. Her sweet, hot tongue made the first foray between them, and another jolt slammed through him, a thousandfold more intense than the first. His reaction was so powerful he couldn't move, or else he would have lain down with her there, bared their bodies and made love to her with granite as their bed.

But since he couldn't move, the kiss stayed only a kiss, his hands rested only on her shoulders, and the chastity of body language was what defined and contrasted and elevated that kiss to an intimacy he had never, ever known before.

But after its zenith, before its end, the sound of snow crunching underfoot made his blood run hot and his heart stop cold. Then, too late to respond, too late to take back the long, poignant, idiotic moments of inattentiveness, he heard a familiar voice complaining in a quite cranky tone.

"Thorne, Calder, the both of you have just ruined all my fun."

Chapter Thirteen

"I've got this broken piece of mirror, see, and I wanted to catch your attention with it coming up the valley."

J.D. parted from Ann and turned as she turned, dumbstruck, toward the joking voice. Leaning negligently against the trunk of a tree towering a hundred feet into the air, Matt Guiliani stood sucking on a cedar toothpick, palming a piece of mirror.

Behind him a few steps, his hair the precise shade of Ann's, his wide gray eyes filled with teenage skepticism, stood her son Jaz.

"Guili." Relief swam against the tide of adrenaline in J.D.'s blood. The two of them started for each other, closing the distance until they could shake hands and then embrace in a fierce bear hug.

Ann stood stock still, in fear of saying the wrong thing and in wonder at the sight of this tall, skinny, handsome, angry boy. Her baby.

Hers.

She had never thought of him in any other way. She had kidded herself, told herself, warned herself, but she had never believed he was anyone's baby son but hers. She couldn't breathe, couldn't even think of what to say with her mouth still wet from J.D.'s kiss and her heart still racing and her body still quivering with needs held too long and too fiercely at bay.

Jaz relieved her of the need, turning away and refusing to look at her.

Her eyes darted helplessly to J.D. Not another word had been spoken between him and Matt while she and Jaz stared at each other. J.D. turned to Jaz, took the few steps separating them and offered her son his hand. "You must be Jaz."

Jaz blinked. His Adam's apple bobbed furiously, giving away emotion, but his voice rang true and deep without a crack, only disdain. "You must be Thorne." His hands were jammed deep into his pockets. He'd no intention of shaking, instead jerked an elbow at Matt. "He said you were pretty smart. He said you could take care of her, but I guess it isn't true since we didn't even have to sneak up on you making out with her."

Caught so clearly out, J.D. angled his head as if to admit to the damning charge and lowered his hand. Matt stuck his hands in his own pockets. Ann wiped tears from her eyes.

Jaz was the one who couldn't take the silence. "Isn't anybody going to say anything?"

J.D. met the boy's trenchant look head-on. "You're right. I screwed up looking after your mom—"

"She isn't my mom." His lower lip jutted fiercely. "What kind of mother abandons her own kid?"

"Suppose you put a lid on the attitude till you know all the facts."

Jaz clamped his teeth together, daring J.D. to do

anything to him. "All the facts in the world don't change her running out on me."

J.D. straightened, looked more menacing, bent on forcing some mote of respect for her. She couldn't bear it.

"Leave him be, Thorne." She could have died, wanted to die under her son's scathing refusal to even look at her.

Matt cleared his throat, reached up and took the toothpick from his mouth. "Suppose we get out of the open and go where it'll be safe to talk. We've been hanging out waiting for you in a cave a couple hundred yards up the hill."

Jaz turned around and walked off. Matt gave Ann a hug. "Don't worry. He'll come around, Ann. Thing is, he's pretty shaken up now."

She backhanded one last tear. "Who wouldn't be?"

"Exactly."

She took a tissue from her coat pocket and dropped back in her tube of lip gloss. "I can't believe you're the one with Jaz. We've been so panicked thinking the TruthSayers had gotten hold of him."

"They almost did, Ann. The bad guys followed him out of Billings. They were closing in to nab him when I just happened to stop for gas outside of Ranchester, and there was the yellow T-Bird."

"You were the teacher, then, who talked to Roy Burgess?"

"One and the same," Matt acknowledged.

J.D. mimed shooting himself in the head. "We knew the old codger had been vetted by a pro. I should have known it was you. So you also snatched him right out from under their noses?''

Matt grinned. ''That would be me too. Come on. We can fill each other in on the way back up.''

Ann retrieved their gloves, J.D. the backpack, and the three of them started trekking up the hill after Jaz. She couldn't wait. ''How did this…how did you find him? How did you know to look? What—''

''Long story,'' Matt interrupted her, giving her a hand up a slippery part of the slope. ''The short and sweet of it is, Rand called me hoping I knew where the two of you had gone, then he called me again to get me to go in with some marshals to get you out. He told me exactly where you were.''

Ann and J.D. traded looks. She shook her head and shrugged, picking her way over tree roots and rocks buried beneath the snow. ''Why would he tell Matt where we were unless he really wanted to help you?''

In the lead, J.D. blew off a frustrated sigh. ''I don't have a clue anymore.''

Matt socked him on the shoulder as they came into sight of the narrow cave opening Jaz slipped into. ''We'll figure it out.''

Inside the cave, there were a battery-operated lantern and some softly glowing coals, the remains of a small fire built inside a circle of stones. Matt credited Jaz for knowing how to tell that the cave also had a natural flue for the smoke to disperse through. ''We've only burned a fire at night so the smoke wouldn't give us away. You two didn't do so poorly yourselves, tracking us down. I hope the badasses aren't as good.''

Jaz dropped loose-limbed into a sulk against the

darker wall. Ann slipped out of her coat and went to him, sinking down on her heels. "Jaz." Her throat clutched. He wouldn't look at her. Tears pricked behind her eyes. "I'm sorry for what's happened to you. I hope you'll forgive me someday, but I wouldn't think of asking that now. The thing is, we need to work together, because the men who torched your house and killed your parents—"

"They weren't my parents either," he uttered, half-sullen, half in denial that he had cared for them or suffered their loss still.

She remembered only too well the keen stab of remorse and loss, of running away, cutting herself off from her family and her colony, the only love she had or knew. "I know what—"

"You don't know squat," he interrupted, accusing her with his first look at her as well.

"You don't know squat about me, either, Jaz, but whether you believe me or not, I have always loved you. You won't accept that now, and I don't blame you. All I'm telling you is that unless we all work together, none of us will come out of this alive."

"I don't have nothin' to do—"

"Anything to do, you mean?" She gave a smile he wouldn't return. "You do, Jaz. You can tell us what happened, and maybe then we'll know who did this and how to protect ourselves."

"I don't know what happened."

She could see that he was not thawing, only uncertain. She wanted to take him in her arms as she had hundreds of children over the years in her shelter, but he was still filled with an understandable anger at her, and he might be for a long time. Her throat tightened again. Tears were a blink, a heartbeat away.

She would not cave to them, making herself out to be the victim of her own wrongdoing, when it was Jaz who had suffered the years with parents to whom he had understood instinctively he did not belong.

"Will you come sit with us and we'll try to figure this out?"

"Fine." He shot up and walked to the cave entrance, nearer the natural light where Matt and J.D. had silently waited it out for them.

Ann sat down on the folded sleeping bag J.D. had gotten out for her. The two men just sat crouched on their haunches. She breathed out. J.D. rubbed familiar small circles in the small of her back.

"So you knew roughly where we'd gone from Rand?" he recapped.

Matt nodded. "I decided to go to Cold Springs on my own. It wasn't tough figuring where the redneck TruthSayers hang out." Ann understood him perfectly. After so many years of tracking and dealing with TruthSayers, J.D., Garrett and Matt had an instinct for finding them.

"So I was at this honky-tonk bar and this strange-looking guy comes in."

"Samuel?"

"Never heard his first name. Is he Pullman?"

"Yes."

"Well, the local yokels were having a grand old time getting him liquored up. He started talking and it didn't take long to get the gist of his story." Once Matt heard J.D.'s name, he'd known Annie Tschetter must be Ann, and that she must have taken J.D. to the colony Pullman came from. "I pumped a couple of other guys there till I understood what the colony thing was all about. After a while, Pullman was talking about Annie having betrayed him and run off to Billings to have another man's baby.''

Though he kept looking out the cave entrance, it was clear to them all that Jaz was hanging on every word. Matt described arriving at the Zimmers' already burning house maybe only thirty minutes too late to have tried preventing the carnage. After he caught up with Jaz and the two of them ditched the TruthSayers Matt believed was tailing him, they'd followed Jaz's original plan to head to Hole in the Wall country.

Jaz, however, really didn't know and hadn't seen anything or anyone. He'd been at a friend's house watching TV when the local station had interrupted with news of the hour-old firebombing, and that Jaz himself was suspected of having done it.

J.D. dragged a hand through his hair. ''I wish the hell I knew what had started all this.''

Matt grimaced. ''Are you telling me you don't know?''

''He was injured pretty badly, Matt,'' Ann explained, ''with a bullet that skipped off the armhole of his Kevlar. What clinched it, though, was that he was slammed up against the glass wall of the phone booth. He had a hematoma the size of a child's fist on his head. A terrible concussion. He didn't even begin to remember what had happened earlier in the day until maybe the last twenty-four hours.''

Matt looked at J.D. as if asking if he were still unclear. ''What do you remember now?''

''I'd been to see Rand—''

"He told me that when he called," Matt confirmed.

"Did he tell you I all but accused him of sabotaging any more prosecutions against the TruthSayers?" Matt shook his head. J.D. went on, explaining the strategy Rand had described. "But as Ann pointed out to me when I began to think he was behind all of this, there's no way Rand would be threatened enough by me knowing he'd handed the D.A. an escape hatch. Now you tell me he's the one who leaked where we were to you, which he wouldn't have done unless he really was trying to help us."

"True enough," Matt agreed, "but factor this in. What Rand told me—and remember, I've never even met the guy, barely remember this federal district court judge is a friend of yours—was that you'd accused him of having something to do with John Grenallo's suicide. As in," he paused meaningfully, "it wasn't suicide at all. What I'm here to tell you is, Grenallo didn't kill himself. He was fed some powerful allergen, he went into shock and died, and then he was strung up in his own garage as if he'd hanged himself."

J.D. rocked back on his heels, whistling softly. "Who knew that?"

"Besides the killer?" Matt asked. "Three of us. The medical examiner, our new boss—the assistant U.S. attorney who replaced Grenallo, and me. When Rand told me that, in the context of how paranoid you were, how screwed up your thinking was, I thought maybe you'd come across some independent evidence that Rand was the killer. You're telling me that whatever it was you said to Rand was a stab in the dark?"

"That's what I'm telling you."

Matt stared at him, then looked at Ann, angling his head toward J.D., amazement all over his glamorous Latin-lover features. "You think the guy will ever learn to take credit for having the instincts of a barracuda?"

"Yeah, that's me," J.D. complained. "Tell me what brilliant instinct it was to take this mess to Ann's doorstep."

"She saved your life, didn't she?" Matt retorted. "In my never-humble opinion, whatever keeps you alive is by definition brilliant."

Jaz interrupted. "I think there's some dudes coming up here, following your tracks."

Matt and J.D. were instantly on their feet. J.D. snatched the binoculars out of an outer pocket on the backpack and focused out the cave opening where Jaz pointed. Ann scrambled up and began shaping the sleeping bag into a tight enough roll to pack again.

Matt dumped a canteen of water on the remaining coals, asking, "You see anything?"

"Yeah. Jaz is right. There's three of them at least, maybe half an hour away on foot."

"There's a helicopter too," Jaz croaked. "Hear it?"

Matt swore under his breath. "I take it all back, Thorne. What'd you do, leave them bread crumbs?"

J.D. shot him a look. "Any bright ideas, spinmeister?"

Jaz cleared his throat. "I know how to get out of here."

Zipping up her coat, Ann gave her son an encouraging nod. "How, Jaz?"

"There's a back way out. I found it looking around last night."

She gave him a broad smile. "Good for you!"

He shrugged, as unwilling as J.D. to take credit. "Stood to reason. You know this is outlaw country. They couldn't go holing themselves up somewhere they couldn't get out of."

But now the whapping noises of the helicopter blades were growing louder. "Best beat it out of here," J.D. said. He gave her son an admiring look too. "Lead the way, Jaz."

The lanky teen grabbed up the lantern and trotted off into the dark, lighting the way. The three of them followed him through a tortuous maze of chambers and narrow passages. J.D. had Ann by the hand. She learned, in those long, nasty moments that she really, really hated dark, close places.

It seemed as if they were only going deeper and deeper into an impenetrable darkness they wouldn't be able to find their way out of. Matt asked only once if Jaz was sure he could remember how to get to the way out he'd found.

"Found my way back, didn't I?"

Which wasn't the same thing at all. But as Jaz began to sidestep along a particularly narrow ledge, the light fell away to nothing, failing to illuminate the depths of the cavern, and the air around them seemed to echo even their breathing. Ann began to hyperventilate.

A black, obliterating panic seized her like nothing she'd ever experienced before. She snatched her hand from J.D.'s and sank to the cold hard ground short of the ledge.

"Ann?"

"You go ahead." Her voice splintered. "I'll find my way back. I'll…" She stared into the pit of blackness, cursing herself, but she couldn't. Couldn't move, couldn't breathe. "I can't do this," she choked out.

J.D. kept offering his hand, but his voice commanded her. "I am not leaving you here, Ann, so get off your butt and give me your hand and do this."

Jaz got safely across to where the ledge widened to at least eight feet. He held the light for her to see. "It's only a little ways, see?"

She couldn't look. "J.D., please go ahead!" she begged. "I'll be okay. You go ahead. Dammit, J.D., go on! You two take Jaz and go!"

"I'm not going either, then," Jaz announced defiantly.

She couldn't help it. She jerked her head up and looked across what seemed to her a chasm at the tears glittering in her son's eyes, illuminated by the lantern he put down beside him.

"I'm not," he warned, his chin wobbling with anger and something almost like love. "Not if you won't come too. You *left* me," he cried, "'n you just better not think I'm gonna leave *you!* I'm better than that!"

She clapped a hand over her mouth to stifle her cry, but it was only half enough, half soon enough. Even the silence echoed itself after her aborted sob fell away. She looked at the impossibly narrow ledge and looked at her son and then J.D., who offered her his hand in a silent entreaty, and in love, again.

"For Jaz," he murmured. "Do it for Jaz, Ann."

She forced herself to her feet, battling an overwhelming feeling of vertigo and shame. What she had done over fifteen years ago had led her to this place and time and desperate situation, and her only remedy lay ahead of her, not behind. A massive shudder gripped her, but she gritted her teeth and gave J.D. her hand.

"That's my girl. You can do this, Ann. You can do it. Just put your other hand against the wall behind you. I won't let anything happen to you."

She stared at the ledge. Her mouth dried till her tongue felt wooden, stiff with fear. Interminable seconds passed.

Jaz's voice cracked as he cried. "C'mon, Mom. You can do it."

Mom. C'mon, Mom. You can do it. Her heart simply melted, simply gathered together again with whatever strength it was that made mothers able to do whatever they had to do, when and how and where they had to do it for their offspring.

She cleared her throat as if it would help and began her journey from a girl who'd given up her beautiful baby son to the woman who was his mother.

At the far end of it, which could only have taken her thirty or forty steps, Jaz took her in his arms, out of J.D.'s, and squeezed her as tight as she could ever have dreamed.

"I hate to break up this little reunion," Matt wisecracked, "but might I just point out that we have to get the *hell* out of here?"

THE FOUR OF THEM split up in the narrow canyon where the shadows were so steep that although the chopper was making reconnaissance sweeps, they could not possibly be seen.

Matt and Jaz headed east. At nightfall they would

use Matt's cell phone to call Hanscomb's service station and beg a ride back out of the canyons. Ann and J.D. lit out going due west by the sun, deeper into the Bighorn Mountains. The plan was incomplete but as good as it was going to get. However it was that they'd been found together with Matt and Jaz, they could avoid detection long enough to escape until Matt could rally help from Garrett and they could confront whatever threat came at Ann and J.D.

All they had to do was stay alive long enough to find a safe haven again and get their GPS coordinates onto Matt's voice mail.

At three o'clock Ann turned around for one last glimpse of Matt and Jaz, but they were already out of sight. At ten after three, as they climbed to higher and higher elevations, the helicopter appeared again as if out of nowhere and hovered nearly on top of the trees, repeating search patterns, coming so close on three separate passes that though they could not be spotted for the forest of trees, they had to cover their ears and could feel the massive rotor blades slicing through the air.

At five, as the last rays of the sun lit the clouds to a brilliant orange from the west, the chopper returned. Near exhaustion, they had come within a hundred yards of a summit where trees no longer grew.

They must have been spotted. Gunfire ripped along the tree line in explosive bursts, and as the chopper dared fly lower, the angle of firepower bit into the trees all around them. J.D. grabbed Ann's hand and despite the forty pounds in the backpack he had on, dragged her faster than she could run downhill, back deeper and deeper into the forest.

Their lives now hung by the slimmest of threads, the desperate hope that the chopper dared not land in the thin mountain air in the ever-deepening twilight.

Chapter Fourteen

At a point perhaps fifty yards into the forest, Ann slipped on an icy patch of the forest floor. Her hand ripped out of J.D.'s grasp and her arm jerked hard in its socket as she fell forward, tumbling head over heels. A thicket of winter-bared scrub oak finally broke her fall, badly scraping her face and hands.

The chopper noises roared just as loud, maybe louder for her own lack of breathing. Bullets still rent the air, bit into trees, ricocheted off the granite outcroppings. The air had been knocked out of her lungs and the stabbing pain of it made her gasp like a fish trapped in shallows.

"Ann!" J.D. called, half sliding, half running down the treacherously icy slope till he reached her. He sank to his butt, turning her, pulling her carefully into his arms, hunching his body around her to protect her from bullets flying thick as deerflies in the summer. "Ann."

All she could think was that her name was again a prayer in his voice. A few lines from the Bible, her favorite from the Song of Songs, poems she had never read inside the colony, came into her mind.

I am my Beloved's and his desire is for me... Set me as a seal upon thine heart.

Desire was what she saw, lust, but far from only that. She saw tenderness and respect, admiration and rage on her behalf, the quality of abiding love, and she knew that if ever she were to be any man's bride, she would be his and only his. If only...if ever.

Tears welled up in her eyes. She could see he thought she must be more hurt than her fall had truly caused. He pulled her hand gently away from her face to see what damage had occurred, to look into her eyes and against her purpose, to see what love was there for him.

His chin trembled uncontrollably, tears filled his beautiful brown eyes. ''Ann.''

''I'm all right, Thorne.'' If she were dying, his beloved, whiskered face was the last sight she ever wanted to see. ''I'll be all right. It doesn't hurt that much.''

Miraculously the sun went down as if between one heartbeat and the next. Bullets stopped flying and the whapping beat of the chopper blades in the air began to fade. He nodded and then helped her to her feet, waiting to see if she had underestimated what toll her fall had taken.

When he knew she was steady on her feet, he began guiding her in a slower, still-relentless descent down the mountain. They would not survive the night in the open. They had to get to a place where there was some shelter from the extreme temperatures made only that much worse by the wind.

Deep in the forested land, just where a treeless meadow began, J.D. spotted in the moonlight what appeared to be some kind of lean-to. Even if that was all the cover it provided, they would have to make do, for the snow in the meadow was hip-deep. They weren't equipped to cross it, or left with the stamina to find a way down that skirted the natural bowl. But within a few steps of the wooden structure, J.D. exulted. The place was a small cabin, little more than a line shack ranchers used for cover and storage of equipment in the high country.

This one had a stovepipe coming out the roof, which meant it would also have a small fireplace or potbellied stove.

The shack wasn't even locked. Inside half an hour, he had a fire going in the stove from wood chopped and left on the north side of the small cabin, and a pot of water heated to boiling from pristine snow she had collected outside.

When they had stripped down to what clothing wasn't wet from snow, underwear and her thin camisole, J.D. spread out the sleeping bags on the crude wooden floor, sat cross-legged on one of them and gathered her into his lap. With a cloth dipped in the water, he began to stroke clean the scratches on her face.

His eyes worshiped her, his tenderness stole from her what guardedness she had left. For long moments, there shimmered an awareness more rare than the blue moon that shone in through the lone window opposite the potbellied stove.

Her head came to rest against his warm, naked chest. His hand cradled her neck, his thumb stroked the uninjured line of her jaw. Her ankle throbbed though she hardly knew it, and the scratches on her face felt raw, but it was the reverent touch of his overlarge hand and callused thumb that brought her a curious peace, edgy with a desire she could scarcely contain.

In all the nights in her lonely bed, she had never dared imagine what would happen if she came to this fluid aching desire deep inside her again, a woman and not a needy, curious hellion of a rebellious girl feeling her oats, witless and knowing nothing of love.

And now the feeling was upon her. Hard upon her, where there were no creature comforts, no satin or candlelight, no violins, and no end to the ways and manners in which she wanted to take him...

...and to be taken by him.

I am my Beloved's and his desire is for me.

She wasn't witless now, and she knew love. Still she had no idea that she had spoken the words aloud, except when he eased her head down onto his arm and propped himself up and looked into her eyes and asked her to repeat what she had just said.

She knew she shouldn't, knew she should never have let the line of poetry into her conscious thoughts at all. Why wasn't it clear to him that her track record, her chain of broken commitments, from the only family she had ever known, to her community and then to her baby son, made loving her one lousy proposition?

And so instead of *I am my Beloved's,* she obeyed that elder's voice inside her head with what she said, "Thorne, you have to stop. You have to. Don't you get it? Don't you see? All I know is how to run from loving anyone!"

He closed his eyes, shook his head, stroked stray strands of hair from her forehead. Firelight danced magically in his hair, made a halo as if he were her guardian angel. "Might as well warn the swallows off Capistrano, Annie Tschetter. I heard you the first time. *I am my Beloved's.* I heard it.''

''You don't know—''

He silenced her protest with his lips pressed hard to her mouth. He would not hear her, would not let her say what had to be said, but the need that had only run like sap in winter for all these years heated inside her and coursed through her body as if no thicker than water.

She gave herself over to his kiss, to answering his lips with hers, his tongue with hers, his urgency with a necessity that brought her to offer her neck to the hungering, gentle bites of his teeth into her flesh. His fingers stole up from her waist, grazing her breast beneath the simple cotton camisole, till they met with his lips on her shoulder and he pulled aside the strap and touched his tongue to her flesh, tasting, slipping ever downward till he suckled her hardened, aching nipple through the fabric that she tore away herself out of sheer desire.

The violence of it, the extremity of tearing her own garment to make way for him drew a primitive, un-civilized groan from him. ''Oh, Ann. I love you, I love you, I love you...''

His words sank like a knife's blade through her intentions, killing the desire in her. She wanted him now so that if she died tonight or tomorrow or the day after that, she would know what it was to make love with a man she loved with all her heart and soul. But she could not go there, could not take his seed inside her, or even his hardened flesh, for so shallow and trifling and selfish a reason as that. J. D. Thorne deserved more than that.

Better than her.

She begged him to stop, and from the torment in his eyes, she knew he knew she meant to include not only making love to her, but loving her at all.

He lifted himself on his arm away from her. He could not believe what she asked of him, couldn't stand to think she could believe him able to do her bidding.

He could never stop loving her.

Barely able to stop the physical expression of his feelings, he turned away from her and sat up, easing his arm from beneath her head.

His broad muscled back made a dark cloud of a silhouette against the light of the fire in the stove. His voice was so low, so harsh she could hardly hear him. "I guess you can take the girl out of the colony, but you can never take the colony out of the girl, huh?"

Tears clogged her throat. "I don't know what that means." But she could guess.

He looked back at her, all the pain he couldn't hide glittering in his eyes. "It means you might as well never have run away, Ann." He had to grit his teeth to keep the trembling of his chin under control at all. "You're a far more efficient jailer to yourself than your elders could ever have been."

He waited, his eyes never leaving hers, wanting an answer of some sort from her, an answer to which she couldn't even fathom the question.

He put it into words too simple to mistake. "What is your freedom worth to you, Ann, if what's between us isn't worth at least as much? Do you imagine that I want you to be anyone different than who you are?"

"I don't even know who I am, Thorne!" she cried.

"I gave away my baby, and I thought I was at peace with that, that I had done for him the best that I could do. But I was wrong. I was selfish. And when he called me Mom today just to snap me out of that ridiculously stupid panic attack, J.D., I thought I would die."

"I'm talking about us, Ann—"

"So am I. Don't you see? Before I was ever even pregnant with Jaz, I knew that you can have your freedom, or you can have love, but you can never have both. As long as you want something you can never be free. I thought I knew that I could never trade away my freedom for love, but you make me crazy with wanting you."

Her voice broke and tears fogged her eyes but she couldn't hold it in anymore, what she felt for him, how confused she had become because he was the man he was. "When you tried to save me from myself in Manny's chop shop, a part of me hated you for it because it made me realize how much I wanted to just curl up in your arms and stay there forever, protected by you.

"And when you made my case with Timothy— about how important it is to do what we do—a part of me knew I had already fallen completely in love with you because you would never take from me who I am on my own.

"And when you were asleep, J.D., unconscious, I wanted to make love with you. I would make love with you now, here and now, but you deserve more J.D., and I don't know how to be better than I am. Don't you see, I'm afraid? That I don't know how to promise you more and be certain of keeping the promise?" She reached up to touch his face. "I swear to you, if I ever saw the look in your eyes that I saw in Jaz's this morning, I would die.''

His eyelids drifted down, reveling in her touch, his whiskered face turning against her hand until his lips grazed the mound of her thumb, then her palm, dampening, kissing, caressing, stroking as if, should that be all he would ever get from her, the chance to kiss the flesh of her palm, he would take it.

Guilt swamped her. All her life she had asked life, even God, to deliver her the ability to want what she wanted without the censure of the colony or anyone else. J.D. had not only shown her what she wanted, he offered it to her as well, but she was so addicted to what she could not have that she had made herself into the cause and the enforcer of all the same old prohibitions.

What had she been thinking? If she had set out to break a man's heart—the furthest thing from her mind and heart—she could not have done it so cruelly or so efficiently. She had only wanted to save him from himself, to—

To save him from loving her...

It struck her, then, with more force than the fall that had knocked the very air out of her, that she was doing to J.D. what she had rejected out of hand him doing for her.

Her every effort, save those sweet secret sacred liberties she had taken from him in his sleep, had been aimed at saving J. D. Thorne from himself.

''I'm sorry—''

''Not good enough,'' he interrupted, his anger at her inability to reconcile her heart and mind finally breaking loose, his unwillingness to listen to her apologies or all her belated regrets thick in his voice.

"I love you, Ann. I always will. But maybe we are too different. Maybe I don't know how to change, either. See, you've convinced yourself that you can never be free if you want something. I believe you're not even alive unless you do."

THOUGH HE HAD fallen asleep on his side facing away from Ann, he woke just before dawn, cradling her in his arms. The disparity between his conscious intentions to back away from her and the reality of his own willing embrace made his heart ache.

He'd had his own share of disappointments in love and in life. He was in the thick of one of them now. No matter which way he turned the kaleidoscope of what he knew of the TruthSayers and his own schoolyard friends, the view didn't get any better, only more tortured.

He'd been betrayed over and over again by one or all of them. And he'd come close to getting married only once, to a woman who was his dead partner's widow, but she believed with all her heart that the happily-ever-after part began with the marriage vows. J.D. knew better.

The only kind of "ever after" J.D. believed in was the kind two people spent a lifetime crafting together. Marriage was only the beginning of life's trials… But by her own inquisitive, strong and fiercely independent nature, all the qualities he loved most, Ann had been forced to stand on her own so early and so alone that she didn't know how to share a burden, or the joy, either.

She expected to disappoint him, but he knew now that her fears were more a reflection of her own judgment against herself. He hoped to God that if she prayed, she would pray for a way to forgive herself.

He had to gain some distance. Slipping his arm gently from beneath her head, he sat up, pulled on dry jeans and began stoking the stove. After a while he heard her sit up, sensed her reaching for her clothes. He said good morning, and she answered in kind.

He turned to watch her, to gauge the tensions between them, but his gaze riveted in the dim light of early dawn to a red mark on her shoulder that could only have been put there by his teeth. Desire slammed through him like an avalanche as she searched through one coat pocket and then another, and finally came up with a tube of lip balm.

The mechanism jammed, the bottom wouldn't turn.

A nasty premonition rose up in him and when she twisted harder, the bottom fell out and with it, a miniature electronic beacon of the sort used to locate downed aircraft.

She stared at the thing in her hand with horror. J.D. swore softly, taking it from her, turning the signaling device over and over in his hand. "It's no wonder the chopper broke off pursuit last night." They could be found again anywhere, at any time with unfailing accuracy inside of twenty square yards.

He frowned grimly. "Okay, then. This is how we'll lure them into an ambush of our own."

ANN DRESSED QUICKLY as he explained to her what he had in mind, but then a shout rose up from outdoors, rendering an ambush a moot endeavor. "Hello! J.D.? Are you in there? Thorne?"

He dived for his piece, still holstered beside the sleeping bags. The skies were gunmetal gray, no relief, no hint of the sun breaking through when heavy footfalls landed on the step up to the line shack and the flimsy door gave way. From his crouched position, one wrist braced by the other, J.D. had Martin Rand dead to rights in his line of fire. And Ann stood now at the small grimy window, looking for the least sign of others approaching as well.

Swallowing hard, Rand took one step back. "Take it easy, J.D. I'm alone and unarmed."

Sent in, J.D. thought, as a distraction. If he were planning his own demise, that's how he'd have done it—sent in a negotiator to buy time and provide distraction while a SWAT team was moved into place. In this case, though, it would be TruthSayers sharpshooters.

Ann shook her head to confirm that she could see no one else coming.

Rand pulled off his gloves and shoved back the hood on his coat. "I swear, J.D. I came alone. Can we talk?"

"You'll understand, Marty," he answered, his tone as lethal as his unforgiving stance, "if I'm not inclined to believe you. How did you get here?"

He shrugged. "As it turns out, you're only about a hundred yards off a road leading to a trailhead used for cross-country skiing." Rand's jaw tightened as he looked from one to the other. He had never met Ann, but he didn't ask for an introduction, or bother with it himself. He met J.D.'s hard look straight on. "J.D., listen to me, and this will turn out all right—"

"It's too late for everything to turn out all right, Marty. Innocent people are dead."

"I had nothing to do with that, J.D."

"But you're here speaking for whoever did," J.D. snapped. "Or am I wrong? I've been wrong before, once or twice. Go ahead, Marty. Tell me how wrong I am."

He cleared his throat. "I'm not going to stand here and pretend mistakes haven't been made, J.D."

"Bad mistakes?" he taunted Rand, daring him to use so benign a word to describe what had gone on since the night J.D. was shot.

His fingers splayed, Rand rubbed his forehead with the base of his forefinger, a nervous gesture so old J.D. could remember when their teachers believed it was a crude gesture or secret signal. "All I ever wanted, J.D., was to keep you out of the line of fire."

"Really."

"Yeah, really."

"How about when you arranged for me to get the undercover position on the TruthSayers task force? Was that all about keeping me out of the line of fire?"

"I had nothing to do with the hiring decision, J.D. John Grenallo would have hired you in a split second—"

J.D. swore softly, cutting Rand off, his look only degrees short of murderous. "Don't, Rand. My application made it to the top of the list because you saw to it, and you saw to it so that you would always have the inside scoop on what the task force was doing, when and how we were doing it."

The vast gray leaden skies began dropping fat snowflakes that swirled in and around the broken door, hanging now by only its upper hinge. Sweating profusely anyway, Rand shed his coat and swallowed woodenly. "So I guess you think I've been one of the TruthSayers all along, is that it?"

"One of them, or the most highly placed dupe in town. Somehow, Marty," J.D. said tightly, "I'd rather believe you're too smart to play the patsy."

"Come on, J.D.!" Rand drew in and let go a shaky breath. "Do you really believe I ever took you for such a fool? Name me one instance when what you told me or what I asked you compromised your investigations."

"Oh, I don't know, Marty," J.D. snapped. "How about the time we were denied a warrant to search the safety-deposit box when Christo McCourt's life was on the line?"

Rand's color turned from flushed to ashen. "We never talked during that whole thing. That wasn't me."

"No," J.D. agreed angrily. "It was your tennis doubles partner."

"It wasn't me, J.D." Rand's weary, sweating pale features tightened. "Look, we can argue this all day—"

"How about the night J.D. was shot?" Ann asked softly, her own anger simmering. "He'd been to see you. He'd let you know he knew that Grenallo hadn't committed suicide, that he'd been murdered. When J.D. called from Cold Springs you knew he didn't remember any of that."

Rand hesitated. "Look, J.D., I came here alone. I had to talk myself blue in the face for the chance—"

J.D. cut him off again. "Spare me your travails and get to the point. *Now.*"

Rand shivered hard but the sweat poured off his face, soaked his hair. J.D. had rarely seen Rand out of his own element, never floundering for words. "Look. I was worried about you—from that stellar moment when you accused me of having something to do with Grenallo's death. What was I supposed to do, J.D.? The man committed suicide. If that was an example of your thinking at the time, then—"

"Grenallo was murdered, Marty."

"And then strung himself up?" Rand scoffed.

"According to the M.E., John Grenallo was dead before his body was hung from the rafters in his garage."

Ann couldn't say what J.D. was thinking, but Rand looked truly befuddled to her. His eyes took on a glazed look, and as if his coat were squeezing his life's breath out of him, Rand pulled against the front of it. "If you say so," he croaked, "I'll believe you. But John Grenallo wasn't the kind of man to take the fall, J.D. Not alone. He'd have taken down any number of men with him."

"Men like himself?" Ann interrupted, moving away from the window, purposefully toward Rand, her gun trained on him. Keenly interested in what she was doing, J.D. straightened. "Men who should be taken down, you mean?" she went on as she began to pat Rand down like an ordinary suspect, concentrating on his sides and chest, talking all the while. "The same men whose names kept surfacing in J.D.'s investigations?" She backed off momentarily, then pulled up Rand's sweater and T-shirt, exposing the wires taped in place to Rand's chest. "The same ones Warren Remster won't be taking to trial, exercising his prosecutorial discretion? Men like *you?*'' she concluded, letting go of his sweater and looking to J.D. for direction in light of the wires Rand wore.

He'd understood the moment she began patting Rand's torso, and in the same instant, known what it was that had set his nerves jangling earlier. Rand had been trying to tell them, with his wild-eyed looks and his blatant comment about their guns, that every word they spoke was being heard elsewhere.

Rand refused to look at Ann, to answer her accusations, but he met J.D.'s eyes. ''Thorne, I swear to you, everything I've done in the last week, I've done to protect you.''

''Who was it that firebombed the Zimmers?'' Ann demanded, refusing to be dismissed, feeling as if she would never, ever be closer to pulling the trigger on an unarmed man than she was right now.

He looked at her as if she had lost her mind. ''How the hell would I know that—''

J.D. shot off a round of ammo through the primitive ceiling. ''The next one,'' he warned softly, ''will find the mark. Or is that what they want? Then all their problems will be over, huh? If I go down for your murder?''

Rand's voice quavered, losing timbre, uncertainty eating away at him. ''C'mon, man! I don't know who did what. All I'm asking for is the chance to put an end to a no-win situation here. Give yourselves up to me, we'll get back to civilization, get a hot shower and something to eat and then we can sort it all out.''

''Sort out what exactly? Was it Ames who tried to kill me and then firebombed the Zimmers?'' J.D. asked. ''Or was it all orchestrated by Everly? Is that the kind of sorting out you mean?''

Rand's mouth clapped shut, and then he began to beg. "Come on, J.D. All you have to do is bend a little and this will go away. Don't be a fool."

"These are not paranoid delusions, Mr. Rand," Ann snapped. "Everly is the one, the *only* one, who had the opportunity to put the clever little beacon in my coat pocket."

Rand finally spoke to her. "You know, Ann, I wish you and I had met under different circumstances."

"I'm sorry we met at all."

"My point is," he persisted, his teeth grinding desperately, "your conclusions are beyond the pale! My God, Kyle Everly's got so damned much money there is no way he'd stoop to this! Even if he did, do you seriously think you can touch him?"

J.D. laughed without humor. "That's it, then, isn't it? The reason you're up here? Everly's going to go scot-free while you and Ames bite the dust. What's your deal, Rand? Talk me down from this psychotic episode I'm having and Everly will buy you a plane ticket to some nice little beach in some foreign country without an extradition agreement?"

Rand fell silent for a moment, his head hanging, his shoulders slumped. "I've no intention of going anywhere, J.D. I am a federal district court judge. I am not some thug. I'll ask you one last time. Let it drop. Just let it go."

"I can't do that, Marty. I'm not bending, I'm not backing off, I'm not stopping till that someone pays and pays dearly. And I'll see you dead and buried before I see you resume the federal bench."

"Is that a threat, J.D.?" Rand demanded. "Are you threatening me now?"

"Yeah, Marty, I am, because I don't know that it's a crime to threaten an officer of the court. Maybe you, on the other hand, have forgotten that it's a crime to solicit the murder of another human being." He lowered the gun before he fired it at Rand out of pure rage. "Maybe Ames never fully developed the moral judgment of a slug. Who was it who torched Ida Ames's diner, Rand? Was it Everly, or did Everly make Ames do it? Exactly what happened that night?"

"J.D., that was half a lifetime ago," Rand choked out. "For God's sake—"

"Don't do that, Rand. Not even he can redeem your blackened, miserable little soul."

"Just give it up," Rand begged, "and you'll see. None of us wants you dead!"

"Oh, but some of us do, Marty," came a voice from outside the broken door, in the same instant the barrel of a sawed-off shotgun appeared, trained on Rand's midsection. "It's your ol' buddy Dougie Ames here," he called, "'n I want you to mind your p's and q's, J.D., because our honorable federal district court magistrate here really is the innocent lackey in all of this."

"Ames—"

"Don't even think about it, Thorne," Ames bellowed. "Not another word, or Rand here'll die a very messy death."

Rand trembled violently, pleading with J.D., "Please…do what he says."

J.D. dragged a hand through his hair, stymied, thwarted by a punk like Dougie Ames. Ann backed up toward the window, certain that it was futile to believe she could get a shot off that would stop Ames. He had to be standing just outside the door, flattened to the outer surface as she was to the inside. She sidled near the door, indicating to J.D. that the mirror image of her position was where Ames must be.

"The silence is beginning to make me unhappy," Ames singsonged. Then he snarled, "You and the broad put down your weapons and skid 'em on across the floor and out the door. Then maybe we'll have ourselves a nice little chat."

"You know I can't do that, Ames." J.D. knelt again, braced and readied to take his best shot through the flimsy, weatherworn wall itself. At J.D.'s ready signal, he fired and Ann dived toward Rand to drag him down and out of the line of fire, but in an act of pure desperation and the loyalty he had protested, Rand spun around in the same moment and made a grab for Ames's shotgun. He managed only to bear the muzzle down closer to his body when the hideous blast went off in his gut.

Ann crawled toward Rand, but he didn't live long enough to draw another useless breath. J.D. hurled himself out the door, falling backward to take aim one more time if Ames was still shooting.

Ames, though, had collapsed on his own weapon. J.D.'s bullet had caught him in the chest. Screaming vile epithets, he cursed J.D. to hell through the blood gurgling in his throat.

IN THE COURTROOM of Federal District Court Magistrate Martin Rand, being transferred now to his successor, J.D. delivered a brief eulogy befitting a man who had distinguished himself by his appointment to the bench at so young an age, whose judicial decisions reflected the insight of a keen and compassionate man, and whose loyalty to a true friend had cost him his life.

J.D. missed Rand, grieved their last moments together, for as it turned out, Martin had known nothing. Ames lived just long enough to spew the truth at J.D. in the ambulance he summoned on Ames's cell phone. He'd played Rand better than Rand had played his beloved Stradivarius. Rand had told Ames once, as a matter of practicality and because he loved to expound upon the law, the strategy that would enable the D.A. to drop the remaining TruthSayers cases. Ames passed it along.

Rand got J.D.'s call. Ames was there to take the colony's number right off the caller ID box.

So it had gone, on and on. And what's more, Ames bragged to his dying breath, they would never touch Kyle Everly. Not in a million years. A righteous TruthSayer to the last.

But Ames didn't live long enough to know the word *never* was the equivalent of waving a red flag in the face of a bull where J.D.'s partner Matt Guiliani was concerned.

And though Ames admitted to no crimes, when all was said and done, his prints matched the evidence recovered from the firebombing of the Zimmer home, and the takeout food containers from which the ruined former assistant U.S. attorney John Grenallo had eaten his last meal. Their deaths were avenged with Ames's own, to the extent anyone's untimely death can ever be redressed.

The swearing in of Martin Rand's successor coincided to the day, seven weeks later, on which

Ann's petition for guardianship of Jason Adam Zimmer was to be considered.

J.D. hopped a flight to Billings after his appearance at the courthouse in Seattle. He took no luggage, didn't know if he would be staying, but inside the breast pocket of his suit jacket was the letter Ann had written him from Billings five weeks earlier. He waited until the 727 achieved its cruising altitude, wanting to read her letter surrounded by clouds. The paper gave a delicate scent that made his memory recall those nights in the bookbinder's hut.

J.D.,

Jaz and I are getting to know each other. He's still in school, of course, and he has his friends, people who love him, Zimmer relatives to see. I can never seem to get enough of him, even in his mouthy moods. I suppose I can never make up for the time I gave away.

I've petitioned the family court for guardianship. The hearing is coming up in only two weeks now. Jaz, I think, is not unwilling to come back to Seattle with me. I've told him all about my life there, and while he thinks it's cool that I am a detective, and swell that battered women and children have someplace to go, he really doesn't buy that I have a life of my own.

He's afraid I'll smother him.

I'm not so worried about that. I know what it was to be smothered. I was always afraid even to breathe in the colony, for fear of it being wicked and lustful—an exaggeration, I know, but the truth all the same.

This morning over breakfast Jaz asked me if the guy with whom I was "sucking face" below the Outlaw Cave is "anywhere in the picture."

I told him I don't know.

I didn't tell him I feel like Sleeping Beauty, awakened to a whole new world with your kiss—metaphorically speaking! Awake and alive for the first time because I want Jaz and I want you in my life, and you are the one who set me free to want anything at all.

Jonah David Thorne, this is my petition to you. I love you for your fatal flaw of uncommon loyalty, and for your wise heart, and for your commitment to making this world a better, safer place, and for the way you looked at me in the lamplight when I would take down my braids. Maybe they have something there. What do you think?

Petitioner requests the privilege of your presence in her life. Petitioner seeks no happily-ever-after, only the chance to serve and be served, to love and be loved, to honor and be honored, so long as we both shall live.

I am my Beloved's. Is his desire in me?

In her? Nowhere else, J.D. thought. He wanted all that too.

HE RENTED A CAR from the airport, and drove to the courthouse in Billings. He'd only just turned down the hallway leading to the courtroom of the Honorable Rowena P. Moore when Guiliani poked his head out of the door one last time to see if J.D. was going to make it on time, or what.

The look on Matt's face wasn't encouraging. J.D. swallowed hard. "What's going on? Is it over?"

"All but the shouting. We have a family values judge on the bench, with a single mother petitioning for guardianship of a child she gave up fifteen years ago. It's not good, J.D."

His heart sank. This moment was supposed to be hers, the moment when the mistake of half a lifetime ago would be redressed, the moment a mother and son were reunited in the eyes of the law. Dammit, Ann deserved this. He'd come at this moment and not before only to celebrate with her and then accept her petition to him. "You're telling me—"

Having delayed the undercover operation to settle the score with Kyle Everly, Matt was in no mood for Ann to lose. "In the absence of a spectacular save, my friend, the fat lady sings in about thirty seconds."

ANN SAT with her family court attorney at the petitioner's table feeling numb. Jaz had refused to sit with the attorney representing the Child Protective Services department. He sat behind her, in the second row back, but that was as far as he would go toward committing himself to her.

His only alternative, save a foster home, was the family of a Zimmer second cousin, a woman who home-schooled her children, won blue ribbons at the state fair for her pies, and whose husband was a track coach and scoutmaster. The judge wanted the boy, whose own record demonstrated just as clearly his need for a strong hand, to go to exactly such a two-parent home.

But Jaz belonged with her. She understood that, if no one else did.

She'd written to J.D., before she knew her lack of
a husband and father figure for Jaz might become the
issue. When that became the stumbling block, she
was unable to phone J.D., to hurry him, to ask for
an answer, afraid to confess she would lose Jaz without J.D.

And she was scared now. Scared to glance back
at the small commotion Matt was causing, fearful of
imposing some sense of guilt on Jaz by her expression, even more afraid of indulging any hope of some
miracle occurring.

Her heart clogged her throat, and tears blurred the
stars of the flag in the courtroom. J.D. hadn't written
to answer her. Hadn't called, hadn't even spoken to
Matt about her. If he meant to let her down easy, to
convey that his feelings for her weren't what he'd
once imagined, he would have done it, wouldn't he?
Said the words and been long since done with it? His
honor and loyalty to her, especially if he meant only
to be friends, would have demanded a speedy reply,
the gentle end.

Or so she imagined. Which was what made foolish
hope spring eternal even now at the eleventh hour.
Afraid of her own hope, she didn't see Matt reenter
the courtroom.

"*Mr.* Guiliani," the judge intoned, "the petitioner's time for testimony in her behalf has just ex-
pired. I am ready to render my decision in this case,
and I would greatly appreciate it if you would—"

"Your Honor, if I may?"

His voice. Her name. Her breath caught. When she
thought of his voice, it was her name she heard, spoken like a prayer. But dear Lord…had he somehow

learned she would lose Jaz without him? Had he come only to spare her that loss?

"You would be…?" the judge asked impatiently.

He stood now in line with the lawyers' tables, facing forward. "J.D. Thorne, Your Honor. Jonah David Thorne for the petitioner, and for her son, Jason."

Ann's heart thudded heavily, but the judge rolled her eyes. "Would you do us the very great honor of taking the witness stand? And you, young man—" she wagged a finger at Jaz "—retake your seat immediately."

"But I… This…I mean he's— What's he doing here?"

"Listen, and maybe you will find out." Ignoring the attorneys, the judge looked down on J.D., and swore him in, taking his address and occupation. "Fine, then. We'll forgo the formalities, Mr. Thorne, if you would be so kind as to enlighten us all. Make it short and sweet, huh?"

He looked at Ann then, could only look at her. Her throat thickened with tears before he ever spoke. There was nothing to ignite her worst fear, that he had come out of some misplaced obligation, nothing to feed that panic, nothing vaguely fond or friendly or fickle in his eyes, but something afire.

Something breathtaking.

Something of intimacy and expectation and permanence.

"Your Honor," he addressed the judge, but spoke, heart and soul to Ann, looking into her watery eyes, "the petitioner came to Billings to spend this time with her son, to begin building a life together with him.

''The petitioner didn't want to put her relationship with me at issue here, and I chose to honor her time alone with her son, knowing there would come a time for us—for the three of us—when the two of them had been restored. The short and sweet of it is, Your Honor, that the petitioner and I wish to be married and to become a family.''

''Hot damn!'' Jaz cried, high-fiving Guiliani.

Ann looked back at J.D., could only look at him. Not on bended knee or beneath the stars but in a courtroom from the witness chair, forever in the record, he proposed to accept her other petition. ''Will you still have me, Annie Calder?''

''Ms. Calder?'' the judge asked, not bothering to conceal her amusement, dismissing her confusion. ''What say you?''

Her heart knocked about with a joy too keen to bear. ''Only one thing.'' *I am my Beloved's, and his desire is for me.*

''And that would be what?''

''Yes.''

The judge rolled her eyes again, banged her gavel and granted the petitioner's request.

Looking For More Romance?

Visit Romance.net

Check in daily for these and other exciting features:

Hot off the press

View all current titles, and purchase them on-line.

What do the stars have in store for you?

Horoscope

Hot deals

Exclusive offers available only at Romance.net

Plus, don't miss our interactive quizzes, contests and bonus gifts.

PWEB